SKID MARKS
VISION

GEORGE PA DOVER

OP Books is an imprint of Olai Press, a division of Olai Multiversal Enterprises LLC.

27137 Nudgent Street. Boron, CA 93516

Olai Press, OP Books, WD Books, Blossom Books, and their logos are trademarks of Olai Multiversal Enterprises LLC.

Dover, George P A, 1960—

Skid Marks Vision / George P A Dover. 1st OP Books ed.

p. cm

ISBN: 978-0-9818503-9-9 (alk. Paper)

  1. Pre-slavery Alkebulan — Fiction
  2. Kumasi, Ghana — Fiction
  3. Genetic Memory — Fiction
  4. Alkebulan Spiritualism — Fiction
  5. Trans-Atlantic Slave Trade — Fiction
  6. Dutch & British Guiana — Fiction
  7. Rebellion & Survival
I. Title

Cover illustration done by Kofi Jah G on Canva

Dedicated to my sisters:

Ingrid (posthumously) , Jane, Gracia, Leslyn, and Nathica

ACKNOWLEDGMENTS

As always, all praise and gratitude are due, first and foremost, unto Jah Almighty and my ancestors, all the way down to my wonderful parents. The love and support of my immediate family sustain me through the solitary nights that I stay up writing, researching, editing, revising, and writing even more. So, I say thanks to and for you all!

Much appreciation for Daniela Araujo and her staff at Evolve Brand, a bastion in public relations.

And finally, much love to all my readers!

"Vibration is the frequency with which the universe

communicates; tune in."

– Lucas Bennett

Chapter One: The Ringing

Cassandra Clairborne woke into the smell of antiseptic and the hush of a hospital that never truly slept. For a second she did not remember the bus or the blur of asphalt or the scream that had yanked itself out of her throat. Then the ceiling lights blurred into halos, and her mother's face pressed into view — eyes swollen, smile trembling like a tightrope.

"Hey, Cassie," Mom whispered. "You scared us, baby."

Her father stood just behind, hand on the bed rail, jaw clenched the way it gets whenever he's trying to be a wall. "Took a whole week," he said with a sniff of a laugh. "You sure know how to make an entrance."

A doctor in blue scrubs slid the curtain aside, flipping through a tablet. He looked younger than the worry in his eyes. "Good morning, Cassandra. I'm Dr. Dwyer. How's the head?"

"Feels like a drum somebody forgot to stop hitting," Cassandra said. Her voice sounded like it belonged to someone small and far away.

Dr. Dwyer nodded. "Expected. You've been in a coma for seven days after the crash. Lots of rest, lots of fluids. Your scans look clean. Some contusions — bumps and bruises — but no hemorrhage. That's the good news." He glanced at her parents. "The cautious news: post-concussive syndrome is sneaky. Fatigue, headaches, sensitivity to light and sound, nausea. Cognitive load makes it worse."

Mom shifted. "So, what exactly do we do?"

"No school for a month," Dr. Dwyer said. "No heavy lifting. And — this is going to be the hardest part — no reading, no television, no phone, no computer. Brain rest."

Dad frowned. "No reading at all?"

"None," Dr. Dwyer said. "Think of her brain like a sprained ankle. You don't run on it the next day. You keep weight off so it heals properly. We'll schedule a follow-up in two weeks. If she reports dizziness, confusion, or worsening headaches, you call me or come straight back. Understood?"

Mom squeezed Cassandra's fingers. "We understand."

Cassandra stared at her knees under the blanket. "No phone?" she asked, not whining, just stunned. "What am I supposed to do— count ceiling tiles?"

"Exactly," Dr. Dwyer said, smiling. "Count them. Breathe. Listen to people. Pet your dog if you have one."

"We have a fish," Dad said.

"Then watch the fish," Dr. Dwyer replied. "Low stimulus. Short conversations. Dim lights. We want the swelling to settle and the neurons to stop yelling at each other."

Mom bit her lip. "Is she safe to move? There are…memories she doesn't seem to have."

"That's normal," Dr. Dwyer said. "The brain sometimes protects itself by fogging the edges. Don't force it. Don't quiz her. Let it come back when it's ready." He looked at Cassandra again. "You did a hard thing—coming back. Now we'll protect that comeback. Deal?"

3

Cassandra lifted a thumb and tried a smile. "Deal."

****

At home in the High Desert, the living room blinds were half closed, slicing sunlight into soft ribbons across the couch. Grandma Yvette—Mom's mother—had already rearranged the room to feel like a quiet nest: blankets folded, pillows propped, a pitcher of ginger tea sweating on a trivet. The twins, six-year-old Jordan and five-year-old Maya, danced around the coffee table, attention bouncing like rubber balls.

"Shhh," Mom said. "Quiet feet. Doctor's orders."

Cassandra sank into her corner of the couch. The house carried its usual smells—laundry soap, cumin from the kitchen, the faint dust of the desert that sneaks in no matter how well you seal a door. Dad fussed with the lamps until the light was soft. He set the fishbowl on the side table so the blue betta could drift like a living lullaby.

Jordan climbed onto the ottoman. "We can play cars," he announced, already revving a toy with his mouth. "Or pirates. I got eye patches."

4

"No pirates," Maya said, arms folded. "Cassie is a queen. Queens don't be pirates."

Cassandra tried. She really did. They stacked blocks. They played a version of "I Spy" that turned into "I Whisper" and then into "I Nap, Maybe." But the twins' excitement kept skittering louder, and every sudden shriek shot a pin through her skull. After twenty patient minutes, she pressed the heel of her hand to her forehead.

Grandma Yvette appeared, leaning on her cane like a conductor's baton. Her silver locs were wrapped in a navy headscarf scattered with tiny suns. She took one look at Cassandra's eyes and clucked her tongue.

"Come, chirren," she said to the twins in that lilting Guyanese music that made even scoldings sound like songs. "Let your sister's brain take a little breeze. We go find something quiet for these hands."

"But I wanna show Cassie my skid mark," Jordan said, indignant. "From my bike. Daddy say it's epic."

"Epic can wait," Grandma said, her eyebrows two grey commas. "Cassie needs story medicine."

5

The twins groaned, but they followed Mom toward the kitchen, lured by the promise of fruit and the important work of arranging strawberries by size. Grandma lowered herself next to Cassandra and patted her knee.

"You want a story, meh chile?"

Cassandra's mouth had already formed yes before she thought of what. "Can I...hear one from before-before?" she asked. "From where you came from? Not long-ago like when Mom was little. I mean way-back."

Grandma's smile folded soft as a shawl. "Way-back, eh? All right. Close your eyes. No straining. Just listen." She adjusted her scarf and let her voice settle into its river. "Long before Columbus dream any sea, before even Jesus walk the earth, there was a kingdom along the big bend of the Nile—Kush. Black stone and sun and river. And in that kingdom lived a little girl with eyes like new cocoa. Her mother called she Nahi. One day, Nahi hand in her grandmother hand, they go to the pyramid—tall as a promise, sharp as the first note of morning."

Cassandra's lashes fluttered. The living room faded to a gentle blur; her breath fell into the rhythm of Grandma's words.

"The sand was cool before the day get hot-hot," Grandma said, "and the pyramid side catch the sun slow, like it learning to glow. Soldiers stand quiet. Priests with shaved heads watch the two pass. The doorway open like the mouth of a lion, and inside — eh-eh — darkness like velvet. But not scary darkness. The kind that make you whisper."

Cassandra felt the couch loosen under her until it wasn't a couch but a stepping-stone in cooling sand. The air changed: drier, older. She could smell limestone, sweat, a thin sweetness like crushed date. Grandma's hand was in hers, warm and certain.

They were no longer in the living room. They were at the base of a stone giant.

"Wait," Cassandra breathed. "Are we...?"

"Shhh," Grandma said, not as a hush but as a blessing. "We walking. If yuh try to look too hard, it gon vanish. Let it come."

They crossed the threshold and the temperature dropped a whisper. A torch guttered in a bronze sconce, smoke writing its slow script on the ceiling. The chamber swallowed sound; even their footsteps were careful.

"This first room is for the living," Grandma said, her voice both beside Cassandra and echoing from stone. "Offerings—bread, beer, figs. The dead don't eat like we eat, but the living feed them anyway. Gratitude is a bridge."

Cassandra's eyes adjusted, drawing shapes from the murk: jars with narrow throats, a low table darkened with use, a painted scene of a boat gliding the river. Every color felt aged but stubborn—reds like clay, blues like dusk. She reached out but didn't touch. Something inside her recognized the arrangement the way her fingers know the shape of home in the dark.

"How do I...know this?" she whispered.

Grandma squeezed her hand. "Memory is a river, Cassie. It bend, it flood, it hide in reeds. But it always find the sea."

They moved into the next chamber through a stone mouth made for gods. The walls narrowed, sloping inward like two palms about to clap. Here the air was sweeter with resin. A carved lioness watched them with eyes tipped in black.

"This place," Grandma said, "keep the tools of passage. Shabti dolls to work in the fields beyond. Amulets for the heart to balance

against truth. See that feather? That is Ma'at—
order, justice. If your heart heavy with lies, the
scale tell on yuh."

Cassandra stepped closer to the feather, painted
on a panel of cedar so smooth it might have
been oiled yesterday. The feather looked so
light it could have floated off. She felt a pull in
her chest, that tug of wanting to promise
something and mean it forever.

They climbed a short flight of steep, narrow
steps, each one wearing a groove where
generations of careful feet had worn stone into
memory. The chamber at the top was smaller,
tighter, with a slab in the middle that was not a
bed, not a table, but something in-between—
something holy.

"The burial chamber," Grandma said softly.
"Here the body rest while the soul take the long
road to the field of reeds. The ceiling full of
stars, because what is a journey without the
night keeping you?"

Cassandra tilted her head. The ceiling was deep
blue, scattered with five-pointed stars, some
clustered, some solitary. Her heart thumped
slowly, in time with a drum she could almost
hear. She reached for Grandma's hand and

found it, the old fingers steady, warm, anchoring.

In the corner, a small niche held something she at first mistook for a toy boat. But it was too precise, too reverent. A boat carved from a dark wood with a prow curved like a question and tiny oars that caught the flicker of torchlight.

"That boat carry prayers," Grandma murmured. "Across the river, across time."

Cassandra closed her eyes. The air tasted of frankincense now, and the weight behind her eyes eased as if the pyramid itself had cupped her skull. She felt close to something enormous and kind.

A sound leaked into the chamber like water under a door. Faint at first. Insistent.

ring… ring… ring…

The torch shivered. The stars blinked.

The boat in the niche became a reflection on a TV screen in an ordinary room. The limestone smell thinned into the citrus of furniture polish. The cool stone under her sandals softened into the couch's cushion. The pyramid door was the hallway. The priests were the coat rack and Dad's hanging jacket.

Cassandra opened her eyes to the living room as the phone kept ringing somewhere deeper in the house.

"Stay," she whispered, but she was speaking to the pyramid, to the feather, to the boat that carried prayers. The sound tugged her back anyway.

Grandma sighed, not disappointed, just calm. "A call is a call," she said. "We'll go back when the river deep enough again."

Mom hurried from the kitchen, hands damp from washing strawberries. "I'm getting it!" she called, and the ring cut off mid-note. Voices muffled. A pause. Then her footsteps returned, slower.

"You okay, Cassie?" Mom asked from the doorway, reading the far-off look in her daughter's eyes.

Cassandra blinked, testing the weight of her body in the room. The ache in her head had cooled, like a fever that remembered discipline. "I think Grandma took me somewhere," she said, half amazed, half certain. "Like…all the way somewhere."

Grandma smiled. "Story medicine."

Dad appeared behind Mom, phone in hand, his brow creased. "Dr. Dwyer moved up the follow-up," he said. "He wants to see you in three days. He says it's good—just checking recovery."

Cassandra felt her stomach tip, a shallow dip like the start of a roller coaster. "In a car?" she asked. The words tasted like tires burning on tar. She saw the flash again—the bus window, the smear of sky, the scream.

Mom crossed the room in two long steps and knelt beside the couch. "We'll go slow," she said. "We'll choose a time when traffic's light. We can stop if you need. You won't be alone."

Grandma's hand found Cassandra's again, that same warm certainty from the pyramid's shadow. "Remember the feather," she said softly. "Light heart. Steady breath."

Cassandra let air fill her chest and leave it again. She imagined the narrow steps under her feet, the ceiling full of stars keeping watch. The world had shaken her once, but somewhere inside a boat waited in a niche, and it would carry her where she needed to go.

"Okay," she said, surprising herself with how steady it sounded. "We'll try."

Dad nodded. "Day after tomorrow. Short drive. Just around the block first."

The twins burst back into the room, hands sticky with strawberry juice, two little comets of energy. "Cassie, guess what," Jordan said, eyes wide. "We made a strawberry pyramid!"

Maya held up a plate where the fruit had been stacked into a lopsided triangle that really did look like a tiny red tomb. "It's for you," she declared. "Queens first."

Cassandra laughed, and the sound did not hurt. "Then I decree—" she announced, putting on a voice, "—that all subjects must share the pyramid equally."

They cheered, and for a moment the room glowed with ordinary joy, a brightness no ceiling tiles could count.

Later, when the house settled into its evening hum and the blinds threw soft ladders across the carpet, Cassandra lay awake on the couch and listened to the quiet. She could still feel the stone's cool patience in her bones. She pictured the driveway outside, the car waiting like an animal that needed taming. She pictured the street—sunbaked, straight, bordered by shrubs that threw little shadows like commas.

"Light heart," she whispered to the ceiling. "Steady breath."

The phone did not ring again. Somewhere in the fishbowl, a fin flicked, and a tiny ripple crossed the water like a prayer crossing time.

Tomorrow would be practice. The day after, the drive. And after that—Chapter Two. The first time back in a vehicle since the accident. The road waiting, quiet as a held breath.

Two: The Road Whispers

The morning of the practice trip, the desert air shimmered over the driveway like glass breathing. The family's 2023 GMC Denali gleamed in the sun—bigger than Cassandra remembered, its chrome grin wide and too confident.

Mom opened the back door. "All right, sweetheart," she said softly. "No rush. Just sit in. We'll only go around the block."

Cassandra hesitated on the porch, her legs suddenly unsure which was first. The driveway sloped ever so slightly, and she could almost see the ghost of the yellow bus flicker at the edge of her vision—its windows, its screech. Then Grandma's voice floated back to her: *Light heart. Steady breath.*

She drew in air through her nose, let it out slow, and climbed in, sliding into the middle row between the twins' empty booster seats. The seatbelt clicked—sharp, final.

Dad glanced back from the driver's seat. "You good back there, baby girl?"

"Trying to be," Cassandra said, forcing a small smile. She closed her eyes quickly, before the road could start to move.

Mom reached around to squeeze her knee. "That's enough for today—just a short loop."

The Denali rolled forward. Cassandra gripped the belt across her chest, whispering to herself: "Light heart. Steady breath. Light heart. Steady—"

Dad's voice drifted through the hum of tires. "You know, next month somebody's turning thirteen. I'm thinking we throw a proper celebration. Poolside, maybe. You'll be our guest of honor."

Cassandra managed a half laugh. "I'm the only guest you'll need."

"Wrong," Dad said, grinning in the rearview mirror. "We're inviting the whole crew. The Claxtons, the McKenzies, even Preacher Fred from church if he promises not to bring his guitar."

Mom chuckled. "You love his guitar."

"I tolerate his guitar," Dad corrected. "It's his singing that needs tuning."

Cassandra's smile came easier this time. The laughter filled the space like sunlight. When Dad finally parked back in the driveway, she opened her eyes and realized she had not cried once.

"See?" Mom said, proud and relieved. "You did it."

Cassandra nodded. "Barely."

Grandma was waiting at the door, her scarf a different color but her eyes the same quiet knowing. "Told you the feather would keep you balanced," she said.

****

Two mornings later came the real test — the trip to the hospital. Cassandra slipped into the same seat, middle row again, the twins staying home this time. She did not close her eyes this time; she wanted to see, to measure how much of her courage was real.

Traffic on the northbound 15 crept along like a river too tired to hurry. Cars shimmered in the heat ahead, a mirage that moved but never arrived. Cassandra watched the asphalt slide under them, dark streaks appearing and fading — the long scars of tires that had screamed once and gone silent. Her palms sweated, but she did not look away.

"You okay back there?" Dad asked, glancing in the mirror.

"Yeah," Cassandra said. "I'm… watching."

"Good," Mom said. "That's brave."

The hospital's beige walls seemed kinder this time, almost familiar. Dr. Dwyer met them at the nurses' station, smiling like someone who had been waiting for this exact chapter.

"Cassandra," he said warmly, "I'm glad you could make it. I called you back in sooner for a special reason. Think of today as therapy — not tests. We're preparing your mind for a smooth return to school."

Cassandra nodded, following him into the exam room. Electrodes, monitors, and soft-voiced nurses — none of it scared her now.

Dr. Dwyer flipped through his tablet. "Now, tell me, Cassandra — since the last visit, any headaches? Strange dreams? Hallucinations? Anything unusual?"

Her tongue felt heavy. She wanted to say *I walked through a pyramid with my grandmother.* She wanted to tell him about the smell of frankincense, the whisper of sand. But something told her the doctor's eyes wouldn't see what hers had.

"No," she said simply. "Just... dreams that feel real sometimes."

He smiled. "Dreams are the mind's way of exercising. Perfectly healthy."

The tests ran their quiet ballet — light tracking, reflex taps, color naming, memory drills. Dr. Dwyer grew more impressed with every passing minute. He exchanged glances with his assistant, then with her parents.

"Her brain function is completely normal," he said finally, tapping the screen. "Actually, more than normal. Her pattern recall and processing speed are off the charts. It's almost as if her cognitive wiring sharpened since the injury."

Mom blinked. "So... she's okay?"

"She's better than okay," Dr. Dwyer said, a note of wonder creeping in. "But we'll keep observing her. Sometimes trauma re-routes neurons in remarkable ways."

Dad laughed uneasily. "Like she got upgraded."

Dr. Dwyer smiled. "Exactly. We just need to see how far the upgrade goes."

Cassandra met his gaze and held it, and for the first time she noticed something she hadn't before — the faint hum behind his words, like she could hear the shape of his next sentence before he spoke it. She didn't say anything, but she knew. Something had changed in her, something alive and whispering.

That night, lying awake in the quiet house, Cassandra replayed the drive in her mind — the stretch of freeway, the faded black lines curling across the asphalt like burned calligraphy. She could almost feel the rubber against the road, the split second when friction turned to flight. And then, somehow, she could *see* it — every car, every angle, every consequence — like the road itself was showing her the memory it had kept.

The skid marks weren't just stains. They were stories.

Three: The Doubt and the Data

Dr. Dwyer's call came three days later. Mom answered, her voice traveling through the house like cautious light. "Yes, this is she... Uh-huh... Brain wave patterns? You want to what?"

Cassandra sat at the breakfast table, stirring her oatmeal long after it had gone cold. She watched her mother's face shift between confusion and curiosity.

Mom hung up and turned. "Dr. Dwyer wants to run some advanced tests at the university," she said. "Something about your brain activity being... unusual."

Dad lowered his newspaper. "Unusual how?"

"Not bad unusual," Mom said quickly. "More like — she's showing higher synchronization between hemispheres. He thinks it's worth studying."

Dad frowned. "You mean to make her a lab rat?"

"Not at all," Mom said. "He called it a partnership. He says Cassie's mind might help them understand recovery patterns after trauma."

Cassandra lifted her eyes. "Do I have to?"

Mom softened. "He said it's your choice, baby."

Grandma Yvette, who had been eavesdropping from the kitchen doorway, spoke without turning. "Every gift come with its test. Yuh pass by facing it, not by hiding from it."

Cassandra swallowed the lump in her throat and nodded. "I'll go."

****

The following week, they drove to the University Medical Research Center — sterile hallways, polished floors, and glass walls that reflected light like mirrors waiting for secrets.

Dr. Dwyer greeted them in a crisp white coat, his enthusiasm barely contained. "Cassandra! Glad you agreed to come. We'll be running some noninvasive scans — just measuring brain activity while you rest and while you solve simple tasks."

Mom squeezed her shoulder. "We'll be right outside."

The lab looked like a spaceship—machines humming softly, a ring of monitors pulsing with blue lines. Electrodes were fitted to her scalp, cold and sticky. Cassandra closed her eyes as the hum filled her ears.

"Just relax," Dr. Dwyer said through the intercom. "Now I'll show you a few images—shapes, colors, letters. Tell me what you recognize."

But even before the screen changed, Cassandra *knew* the shapes. The red triangle, the green spiral, the golden curve of an ancient symbol. When each appeared, it felt less like recognition and more like remembrance.

After the test, Dr. Dwyer studied the data with a furrowed brow. He gestured toward the monitor showing a looping waveform. "Her alpha and gamma waves are… well, synchronized in a way I've never seen. Both hemispheres are firing almost in perfect unison, even in rest state."

The assistant blinked. "That's not possible, is it?"

"It shouldn't be," Dwyer murmured. "But here it is."

Mom looked nervous. "What does that mean?"

Dr. Dwyer hesitated. "It could mean her brain found a new equilibrium after trauma. Or... that it's accessing pathways we don't fully understand yet." He caught himself, smiled reassuringly. "It's extraordinary, but not dangerous."

Cassandra tilted her head. "Can I see?"

He showed her the screen. Waves of blue and green crossed each other like braided rivers. She stared, and for a moment, she could *feel* them pulsing inside her — each line a whisper, a memory of rhythm. Something deep inside said: *This is how light thinks.*

Dr. Dwyer cleared his throat. "We'll schedule more sessions, if you're willing. For now, keep journaling anything unusual. Sensations, images, even dreams."

"Okay," she said, though she didn't tell him she no longer needed dreams to see.

****

That night, Cassandra couldn't sleep. The house was still except for the ticking clock and the fish's slow drift in its bowl. Her sketchbook lay open on her lap. She flipped to a blank page, the pencil trembling in her hand.

Go back, something inside her whispered. *The road remembers.*

She slipped out of bed, barefoot, quiet as thought. Her shoes waited by the door like conspirators.

The moon hung low as she walked toward the overpass where the accident had happened. The desert was silent but for the wind brushing through dry brush. Streetlights buzzed like insects.

She reached the spot — the stretch of freeway shoulder where old cones still marked the faded skid marks. They were dark, twisting ribbons on pale concrete, half eroded by weather.

She crouched down, tracing one with her fingertips. Heat shot through her arm — sharp, electric, like memory turned physical.

The world flickered.

In a heartbeat, she wasn't stooping above the marks; she was *inside* them.

Metal screeched. The bus swerved. Tires screamed. A child cried out. She saw flashes — her classmates, the driver's startled eyes in the rearview mirror, the silver blur of an SUV cutting in too close. Every sensory detail poured into her, too fast, too clear.

Then silence.

She gasped and stumbled back, falling onto the gravel. Her breathing came quick and shallow. Her hands shook, but her mind was steady — seeing what others could not.

She opened her sketchbook and began to draw feverishly: the arcs, the angles, the distances between lines. The more she drew, the more sense it made. The marks were not random — they formed a pattern, almost geometric, almost coded.

When she finished, she stared at the page. It was not just the layout of the accident — it was *a blueprint.*

Of movement. Of collision. Of cause.

The wind rustled through the brush. Cassandra looked down at the dark highway, pulse steadying. "You're trying to tell me something," she whispered to the road.

The road did not answer, but the hum beneath her feet said enough.

Four: The Echo Network

It began, as big things often do, with a quiet email.

Dr. Dwyer had intended only to share Cassandra's anonymized data—a string of brainwave patterns identified as *Subject C-74-F*. But the server he uploaded to was not just any university cloud. It was tied to a neuroscience consortium funded partly by government grants, partly by defense research groups that liked to keep their algorithms fed.

By morning, Cassandra's brain had become code: a pattern of light and rhythm traveling across cables, replicated in labs from Boston to Geneva.

Dr. Dwyer didn't know that yet. He was too busy rechecking his graphs, trying to understand why every time he opened Cassandra's scans, the waveform seemed to *shift*, ever so slightly, as though reacting to his attention.

At home, Cassandra felt the first tug of strangeness during breakfast.

Mom was buttering toast. Dad was reading the news aloud in fragments. Cassandra was doodling in her sketchbook—half-asleep, half-dreaming—when she felt it: a faint *pressure* behind her forehead, like the moment before someone says your name.

Then came the whisper—not a sound, but a sense.

"Fascinating synchronization… adolescent female… unprecedented…"

Cassandra's pencil froze midline.

"Cass?" Mom said. "You okay, sweetheart?"

She blinked hard. "Yeah. Just dizzy."

Grandma Yvette looked up from the stove, eyes narrowing. "When the wind change inside your head, chile, it mean somebody calling your spirit."

Dad laughed lightly. "Ma, it's probably just a headache."

But Cassandra wasn't so sure. The whisper had carried *words she didn't know*—scientific words, clipped and cold.

Across the country, in a sterile office lined with glowing monitors, a woman in a navy blazer adjusted her earpiece. "Dr. Merrin," said the analyst beside her, "you need to see this. The Cass-74-F dataset just spiked again—same harmonics, but now the phase coherence is… increasing."

Dr. Merrin leaned in, squinting at the pulsing graph. "Increasing how?"

"It's reacting to observation," the analyst said. "As if it knows we're watching."

****

THAT AFTERNOON, CASSANDRA SAT OUTSIDE on the porch swing, notebook on her lap. The desert stretched out pale and wide, the sky a flat silver. She closed her eyes and listened—not to birds, not to cars, but to *thoughts* that were not her own. She could feel them—clusters of curiosity blooming like sparks in distant rooms. Words floated in half-formed pieces: *subject, synaptic fusion, real-time mapping*. Every thought carried its own color, its own texture—like tasting someone's emotion through glass.

It wasn't noise. It was attention. And it was all directed at her.

She opened her eyes sharply. The notebook page beneath her hand was covered in tight spirals, drawn without memory of moving the

pencil. Each spiral contained smaller ones —
nested, ordered, alive.

Grandma stepped onto the porch, her cane
tapping the boards softly. "Someting stirring in
yuh head again, isn't it?"

Cassandra nodded. "I can feel... people.
Thinking. About me."

Grandma tilted her chin. "Far people?"

"Yes," Cassandra whispered. "And they don't
feel kind."

The older woman lowered herself beside her.
"When a mind shine bright, it draw both moths
and scholars, yuh hear? But light must learn
when to dim."

Cassandra looked down at the spirals. "How do
I do that?"

"You start by not staring back."

****

Meanwhile, at the university, Dr. Dwyer's
inbox began to fill — first one, then five, then
twenty messages.

Subject: Request for Access — Cognitive
Synchrony Study
From: [Redacted]@darpa.gov

Message: "Your dataset exhibits properties of neural entrainment previously deemed theoretical. Immediate collaboration requested."

He rubbed his temples. He hadn't meant for this. He just wanted to understand the girl who had survived the impossible.

He called Mom that evening. "Mrs. Clairborne, how's Cassandra feeling? Any unusual headaches? Nightmares?"

"She's fine," Mom said, though her voice trembled. "Just quiet. Drawing a lot."

"Good," Dwyer said, trying to sound normal. "Tell her I'll check in soon."

He hung up, but the doubt lingered. Something told him Cassandra's data was not just being studied — it was *interacting.*

****

That night, Cassandra dreamed of lights — dozens of them hovering over maps, blinking like patient eyes. She floated above a grid of screens, each showing her own brainwaves, pulsing to the same rhythm.

Then a new thought—not hers—cut through the hum: *"If we can isolate the resonance, we can reproduce it."*

She jolted awake, drenched in sweat.

The digital clock glowed 2:34 a.m.

Her head buzzed. She could feel invisible hands tracing the edges of her mind, searching for an entrance.

She whispered into the darkness, "Stop listening to me."

And somewhere, halfway across the world, a monitor flatlined for exactly one second before resuming.

By the next morning, Cassandra knew this wasn't just curiosity. Someone—or something—was trying to read her as much as she was reading them.

In the reflection of her window, her own eyes flickered with the faintest shimmer of static. She placed her hand against the glass and murmured, "If you're going to look inside me… then I'll look back."

And with that, the feedback loop began.

Five: The Pattern Awakens

It began with a notebook page and a flicker of déjà vu. Cassandra sat cross-legged on her bed, the early light slanting across the comforter. Her sketchbook lay open to the drawing she had made at the accident site — dark arcs, looping angles, careful pencil grooves that still felt warm to the touch.

She flipped to another page: the printout Dr. Dwyer had given her, a copy of her brain-wave scans from the university. Waves and colors — alphas, betas, gammas — braiding across the page like rivers in motion. Something in her chest tightened. The shapes were not just *similar*. They were *the same*.

She laid the two pages side by side, tilting them under the sunlight. The skid marks and the brain waves matched line for line, peak for trough, curve for curve. When she overlaid the sketch onto the scan, the fit was perfect — every jagged turn of rubber meeting every flicker of neuron activity. A cold thrill ran through her. The road and her mind were *telling the same story*.

"Mom," she called softly. "Can you come here a second?"

Mom appeared in the doorway, still in her robe, coffee steaming in the cup in her hand. "What's up, sweetheart?"

"Look," Cassandra said, holding out the two sheets. "See this? The road I drew and the scan from Dr. Dwyer — they line up. Exactly."

Mom leaned closer, squinting. "Honey, that's just… coincidence, isn't it? Curves look similar sometimes."

Cassandra shook her head. "No. Watch." She slid the transparency of the scan over her drawing again, aligning the edges. "Every line matches. Every single one."

Mom hesitated, the coffee cooling in her hand. "Cassie, maybe you've been thinking about the accident too much. Sometimes the brain connects things that — "

"I didn't connect them," Cassandra interrupted. "They connected themselves."

Mom's eyes softened, worried. "Why don't you rest a bit, hmm? You've been through so much."

35

After her mom left, Cassandra exhaled through her nose, frustration bubbling beneath her ribs. Adults always tried to shrink the impossible until it fit their comfort.

But she could *feel* it pulsing between the two papers — a magnetic resonance, a hum like the edge of a thunderstorm. She pressed her fingers against the overlay. The air around her vibrated. And then, for an instant, she wasn't in her bedroom anymore.

****

SHE WAS STANDING ON THE FREEWAY AGAIN, the wind heavy with the scent of rubber and ozone. The skid marks glowed faintly, luminous under an invisible sun. They curved not randomly but in deliberate patterns — fractal shapes spiraling outward from a single origin point, just like the synaptic bursts on her scan.

She heard Grandma Yvette's voice, distant yet near: *"When two worlds mirror each other, chile, that's how the veil gets thin."*

The air shimmered, and within the glowing lines, she saw *motion* — the replay of the accident, yes, but also something else. Each car's movement followed a rhythm, a kind of pulse. It wasn't chaos; it was choreography. She

36

watched the bus skid, felt the surge of fear again—but beneath that, another current, deeper and calmer. A field of invisible geometry guiding everything toward its exact outcome. When she blinked, she was back in her room. The papers on her lap still hummed faintly.

Later that day, Grandma found her at the kitchen table, tracing the lines again with a pencil tip.

"Yuh found it, eh?" Grandma said quietly, setting down her teacup.

Cassandra looked up. "You knew."

"I didn't know the shape," Grandma said, easing into a chair, "but I knew it would show itself. Life leave fingerprints, even on the air. Yuh got both—mind and world marking each other."

Cassandra frowned. "But why me? Why this?"

Grandma tilted her head. "Because yuh listened when everyone and everything else was screaming." She reached for the papers, fingertips brushing the edge of the drawing. "What yuh see here, that pattern—it's an echo. Of the accident, yes. But maybe also of what was waiting to wake up in yuh."

Cassandra traced one looping line with her fingernail. "It's like… the road and my brain remember the same moment."

"Memory ain't just in people," Grandma said. "The earth remember too. Every wheel that spin, every cry that fly out—it stay. Some folks just know how to hear it."

That night, Cassandra spread both pages on the floor and connected her phone to take pictures. When she zoomed in, she saw even more — microscopic distortions that seemed to form symbols, almost letters, hidden in the crossings of lines.

Then came the pulse again, subtle but insistent, running up her arms like static. She shut her eyes and *saw*—this time not the accident, but herself on the hospital bed, her brain firing patterns that spelled out those same invisible letters. The hum deepened. The air grew warm. When she opened her eyes, a faint light still lingered on the pages—a pattern too precise to be chance, too alive to be ink.

AT THE UNIVERSITY, DR. DWYER STARED at the same pattern on his monitor. The anomaly had resurfaced—Cassandra's latest brain data showing new symmetry, expanding outward like ripples. He rubbed his jaw. "This is… impossible," he muttered. "It's growing."

The assistant frowned. "Growing?"

"Look at the harmonic map," Dwyer said. "The signal isn't static. It's writing something."

"What kind of something?"

He hesitated. "A design."

Back home, Cassandra dreamed of roads twisting into constellations, constellations bending into neurons, neurons branching into pyramids. In every version, the same pattern pulsed beneath—alive, infinite, whispering in a language she almost understood.

She woke with one sentence echoing in her mind, not in her voice but in something older: *The accident was not an end. It was an ignition.*

Chapter Six: The Disruption

The first sign came at breakfast. Cassandra was spooning cereal when the kitchen radio hissed and cut to static. The LED clock on the microwave blinked 12:00, then froze mid-flash. Grandma Yvette muttered a prayer under her breath, and the fishbowl on the counter gave a faint, electric shimmer — the blue betta darted in frantic circles.

Mom frowned. "Power surge?"

Dad checked his phone. "Wi-Fi's dead, too."

Cassandra knew better. She felt it in her chest — the faint vibration she had begun to recognize. The pattern inside her was *pushing outward*.

"Sorry," she whispered, to no one in particular.

The kitchen light flickered once, then steadied.

At the same hour, three miles away, in the basement lab of the university, Dr. Dwyer stared at a monitor that had just gone haywire. Lines of data collapsed into static. The pattern he had been tracking — Cassandra's neural frequency — flared across his screen, bright as a sunburst, then faded.

"Power fault?" his assistant asked.

"No," Dwyer murmured. "That was her."

He pulled up the backup feed — every lab sensor had spiked at the same timestamp, synchronized perfectly down to the millisecond. He felt a chill run up his spine. The building's magnetic compass on the wall twitched, turning a slow circle as if chasing a ghost.

****

Back home, the air itself felt different. Cassandra sat on the porch swing, the pattern pulsing behind her eyelids like a heartbeat that wasn't hers alone. A crow landed on the fence, cocked its head, and began to mimic — not cawing, but echoing faint syllables: *Cass... sand... ra...* The sound snapped her eyes open. The bird flapped and took off, scattering dust. She clutched her sketchbook to her chest. "What's happening to me, Grandma?"

Grandma's voice floated from the doorway. "Yuh tuning the world, child. Every note got its echo."

Cassandra shook her head. "I'm not trying to."

41

"Doesn't matter," Grandma said. "Once a song start, it finish itself."

By afternoon, even the air conditioners along their street were cycling erratically — on, off, on again, the neighborhood hum out of sync. Cassie stood on the front step, staring at the dry horizon where heat shimmered like static on an old TV.

Her phone buzzed unexpectedly back to life. A message from Dr. Dwyer: "Have you noticed anything unusual today? Please call. Urgent."

She hesitated, then dialed.

His voice came fast and low. "Cassandra, listen carefully. Your brainwave pattern is expanding — it's not just localized activity anymore. It's radiating. Every time you focus, every time you think about the pattern, electronic systems within a two-mile radius register magnetic interference."

Her throat tightened. "So… I'm breaking stuff?"

"Not intentionally," he said. "It's as if your consciousness is… broadcasting energy. Like a low-frequency field."

"I don't want to be a field," she whispered.

"Neither do I want you to be studied like one," he said. "I've got colleagues asking questions I can't answer. You need to stay calm, avoid stress, and—Cassandra? Are you still—?"

The line dissolved into static. She dropped the phone. Its screen glowed white, then dimmed to black.

That evening, Dad tried to start the car. It coughed once and died. The dashboard flickered, then went dark. "Battery's fine," he muttered. "This makes no sense."

Mom stood on the porch, arms folded. "It's been happening all over the neighborhood. Power companies don't know what's wrong."

Grandma leaned against the railing. "The air full of her heartbeat," she said softly. "Machines not built to dance to that rhythm."

****

AT THE UNIVERSITY, CHAOS SPREAD through the network. Servers crashed. Compass needles spun in their mounts. The digital clocks on the lab walls froze—all showing the same time: 5:14 p.m.

Dr. Dwyer's assistant stared at the readout. "Sir, it's feeding back. The system's mirroring its own output."

Dwyer rubbed his temples. "It's her resonance. She's synchronizing with our network."

"Can we shut it off?"

Dwyer did not answer. The screens around them brightened one by one, lines of Cassandra's brainwave data weaving together like living calligraphy.
Then the monitors stilled. In the center of every screen, the pattern formed the outline of a single eye — pupil dilating. Watching.

****

At home, Cassandra flinched. Her pulse thudded once, twice. The air thickened. Every phone and TV in the house turned on simultaneously. Static filled the rooms, then her own voice — recorded, fragmented — played back through the speakers:

"If you're going to look inside me... then I'll look back."

Mom screamed. Dad grabbed the remote, clicking it uselessly.

Grandma didn't move. Her gaze stayed on Cassandra. "They looked too deep, baby. Now yuh looking back."

Mom and Dad spoke at once, "Ma, you know what's going on with all this?"

Grandma just looked at them and shrugged her shoulders, then, leaning on her cane, went into the kitchen.

The lights flickered once more — and this time, every bulb in the house burst in unison, showering sparks like tiny stars.

When darkness fell, the hum subsided, leaving only silence and the faint smell of ozone. Cassandra stood amid the quiet ruins of lightbulbs, breathing hard.

"Grandma," she whispered, trembling. "What's happening?"

Grandma's hand found hers. "The pattern awake now. And it hungry to finish what it start."

Seven: The Eyes of the Network

Two days after the blackout, the world around Cassandra began to hum with invisible presence. It wasn't noise exactly — it was *awareness*.

When she stood still long enough, she could feel them: minds, distant and deliberate, brushing against her thoughts like curious fingertips. She didn't know their names. But she knew they were *watching*.

****

Dr. Dwyer sat alone in his office, the blinds drawn tight. His monitor glowed with a message stamped CONFIDENTIAL — FEDERAL REVIEW ACCESS.

He had not meant for it to spread this far. The university's network had automatically uploaded Cassandra's neural scans to an open research exchange before he could stop it. Within hours, he had received emails from half a dozen laboratories and two addresses he didn't recognize — both ending in *.gov*.

Now the data wasn't just his to study. It was *out there*.

A line from one of the messages replayed in his mind:

Subject exhibits unprecedented hemispheric coherence. Recommend immediate cross-analysis for cognitive mapping potential.

He stared at the screen, muttering, "She's not a subject. She's a child."

But even as he said it, another alert appeared — new access detected from an unknown network in Arlington, Virginia.

That evening, Cassandra sat in her room, sketchbook open but untouched. The night pressed against the windows like a held breath. She felt it before she heard it — the faint vibration of *thoughts*, slipping through the static of the world.

Snippets surfaced, as if her brain were tuning a radio with too many frequencies at once:

Pattern expanding…
Subject 74-F receptive to feedback stimuli…

Potential breakthrough — if we can isolate the resonance...

Cassandra clutched her head. "Stop," she whispered. "Get out."

But the thoughts did not belong to anyone in the house. They came from *elsewhere*—from people sitting behind screens, staring at her patterns, thinking her name without knowing her face.

The pressure grew behind her eyes, warm and rhythmic. "Stop thinking about me," she said louder, her voice trembling. The lights flickered in response.

At the same time, in a secured government facility, Dr. Elara Merrin scrolled through Cassandra's data with unblinking fascination.

"Her wave harmonics are aligning with our cognitive model prototypes," an analyst said. "It's as if her brain *knows* the mapping algorithm we've been trying to teach AIs for years."

"Not possible," Merrin replied, though her tone betrayed excitement. "Unless… she's subconsciously reading the data stream itself."

The analyst hesitated. "So, what do we do?"

"Observe. Quietly," Merrin said. "If she's aware of the observation field, we can't risk direct contact yet. The experiment's already running. She's the one conducting it."

****

IN HER DREAMS THAT NIGHT, Cassandra found herself floating in an ocean of light—each wave pulsing with the rhythm of distant minds. She saw faces she didn't know, places she'd never been. Every thought that reached her rippled through the current, and she understood, somehow, that her consciousness had been stretched across the same web that once carried her scans.

She was *inside* the network now.

When she woke, her phone vibrated on the nightstand even though it was not plugged in. The screen lit up—no caller ID, just a text:

Do you feel us, Cassandra?

Her breath caught. The phone buzzed again, the next message appearing on its own.

We feel you.

The screen went black.

Dr. Dwyer was still awake when the same message appeared on his laptop — same words, same sender.

He froze. Then, without thinking, he picked up the phone and dialed Cassandra's house.

"Mrs. Clairborne? It's urgent. I think — "

A high-pitched tone shrieked through the line, cutting him off. Every monitor in his office flashed white for an instant, then returned to normal.

In the silence that followed, he realized what had happened: Cassandra had not just connected to the network. She had *become* part of it.

In her room, Cassandra stared at the black phone screen, heart thudding. She whispered into the dark, "If you can hear me… stop looking. I'm not yours."

Outside, the desert wind shifted direction.

And somewhere deep in the labyrinth of government servers, every file labeled *Cassandra Clairborne* locked itself — access denied, encryption changing line by line — as if the data were defending itself from being read again.

Eight: The Translation

For days, the pattern had refused to leave her mind. Cassandra saw it behind her eyelids, in the whorl of her fingerprints, even in the swirl of milk in her cereal bowl. It wasn't random—it was *speaking*. She spread her sketches across her bedroom floor like puzzle pieces: the skid-mark blueprint, the brain-wave scans, the new spirals she'd drawn in half-conscious moments. The room smelled faintly of graphite and static.

At first glance, the lines looked chaotic, but when she traced them slowly, certain shapes began to repeat—triangular curls, half-suns, clusters of dots that resembled constellations.

Her pencil hovered above the page. "You're trying to tell me something," she murmured.

And then the whisper came—not in words, but in rhythm: three beats, pause, two beats, pause.

Cassandra's heart matched it instinctively. *Three, two. Three, two.* A code.

Grandma Yvette found her like that, cross-legged amid papers and light, the afternoon sun slanting through the blinds in dusty stripes.

"Yuh look like a little scientist," Grandma said softly.

Cassandra didn't look up. "Maybe. But it's not science exactly. It's… language."

Grandma came closer, peering at the drawings. Her eyes narrowed. "Hmm. Those marks… they older than both science and story."

Cassandra frowned. "You've seen them before?"

"Not with these eyes," Grandma said, "but in dreams that smell like sand and old stone. These the signs they carved on pyramid walls back in Kush."

"The same kingdom you told me about," Cassandra whispered. "The little girl — Nahi."

Grandma nodded. "Maybe the same hand that drew them then is holding yuh pencil now."

Cassandra swallowed. The idea both thrilled and terrified her. "But look." She picked up a page and pointed to the lines. "When I convert the angles to numbers — see, 36, 72, 108 — they repeat in perfect ratio. That's geometry, not just art. The same numbers in wave harmonics and sound frequencies."

Grandma smiled faintly. "Yuh finding the bridge between yesterday and tomorrow."

Cassandra looked up at ~~Grandma~~grandmother and locked eyes with her. "How do you know these things and you never even went to co finished high school, Grandma?"

The old matron smiled. "What we have today is not Artificial Intelligence~~,~~, chile. It's Infinite Intelligence. Energy is neither created nor destroyed. "

Later that night, while the rest of the house slept, Cassandra sat by the dim glow of her desk lamp, copying the symbols repeatedly. She began writing the numbers that each shape seemed to hum when she traced it — 3.6, 7.2, 10.8 — until her notebook became a grid of equations.

Then, without meaning to, she began to *hear* them as tones — low, soft frequencies that made her bones vibrate. When she spoke the numbers aloud, the air trembled faintly.

Her phone, sitting on the table, flickered to life on its own. Across the black screen, faint golden

54

letters began to scroll. Cassandra blinked. She did not know the language, but somehow, she understood: *seruwat* — "bridge of breath."

Her pulse raced. "The translation," she whispered. "It's… happening."

****

AT THE UNIVERSITY, DR. DWYER STARED at his monitor in disbelief. The symbols from Cassandra's last scan, which were meant to be pure brainwave readouts, had begun reshaping themselves into geometric clusters. When he zoomed in, he realized they weren't random noise; they were *characters*.

"Looks like proto-script," his assistant muttered. "But nothing matches known databases."

Dwyer leaned closer. "Unless it's not modern at all." He opened an ancient-languages reference window, scrolled, and froze. The match was partial, but clear enough to make his skin prickle.

The lines corresponded with early Kushite-Meroitic inscriptions — forms that had never been fully deciphered.

"She's writing in a dead language," he whispered.

55

"Or rather, a sleeping language whose knowledge she's channeling through her writing," his assistant corrected.

Back at the Clairborne house, Cassandra continued her translation, guided either by logic, by instinct, or the alignment of her consciousness with that of the multiverse. Each pattern seemed to unlock another—symbols unfolding like petals. She filled pages with equations and phonetic notes until her desk looked like an archaeologist's dream.

By dawn, she had written a single phrase in both numbers and letters:

3.6 / 7.2 / 10.8 — *The Mind is the Temple, and Light is the Door.*

Her hands trembled as she copied it again, the air around her thrumming gently, like the first breath before dawn.

Grandma's voice came from the hallway. "Yuh still up, chile?"

"Grandma," Cassandra said, turning toward her, eyes wide. "The symbols—they aren't just words. They're instructions."

"For what?"

Cassandra hesitated. "For remembering how to build the bridge between thought and matter."

Grandma stepped forward, eyes glinting in the dim light. "Then, chile, yuh carry someting the world forgot it knew."

****

MEANWHILE, IN DR. MERRIN'S SECURED RESEARCH FACILITY, a fresh data stream arrived: an unprompted upload from the locked Cassandra file, even though all university access had been revoked. The symbols pulsed across the monitors in gold and white, arranging themselves into the same phrase Cassandra had just written. Technicians stared in silence as the translation auto-rendered beneath:

THE MIND IS THE TEMPLE, AND LIGHT IS THE DOOR.

Dr. Merrin's breath caught. "She's communicating," she said. "Not with us. With the system itself."

That morning, as the sun rose over the desert, Cassandra stepped outside barefoot, her notebook pressed to her chest. The air shimmered, warm and still. Her electromagnetic field recharged from her direct contact with the earth, she whispered the phrase once more, "The mind is the temple. Light is the door."

A faint ripple passed through the world — subtle, almost imperceptible — but enough to make the wind shift and the clouds to part slightly above her head. For the first time, she did not feel like the accident's survivor. She felt like its *result*.

And somewhere, far across the world, lights on servers blinked in unison, acknowledging the message, as if an ancient language had just awakened inside a modern machine.

Nine: The Mystical Parallel

The dream began where memory ended — on the edge of asphalt and eternity. Cassandra stood once more on that stretch of highway where her world had turned upside down. The skid marks — dark, looping, chaotic — ran across the pavement like the signature of something alive. The night wind smelled of rubber and rain, but beneath it lingered another scent — dry earth, myrrh, and something ancient. The lines shimmered faintly in the moonlight. Then they moved.

She gasped as the arcs began to spiral inward, folding into one another until they resembled the coiling hieroglyphs Grandma Yvette had once drawn for her — the spirals of Kemet and Kush, the symbols of the eternal return.

A voice echoed from somewhere within the sound of the wind: *"Every ending leaves a mark. Every mark remembers the shape of its beginning.*

Cassandra sank to her knees. "Who's there?"

"Not who. When."

The skid marks pulsed again, this time glowing faintly gold. The highway melted away, replaced by desert sand and a horizon pierced by a pyramid's shadow. She was both herself and not herself — her body light, her heartbeat ancient. A girl stood before her. Barefoot. Bronze-skinned. Eyes full of knowing. Nahi.

Cassandra's breath caught. "You're the girl from Grandma's story."

Nahi smiled gently. "I am the girl *from your remembering*. We are the same note played twice."

Cassandra looked around — at the pyramid, at the air that shimmered like heat and memory. "This can't be real."

"Reality is only what memory agrees to repeat."

The girl gestured to the pyramid. "You once walked here before your world was made of wheels and wires. The marks you left then still live beneath your skin."

The wind rose.
Hieroglyphs shimmered across the sky like constellations come alive — spirals, suns, and serpents of light twining in rhythmic motion.

The marks sang. Cassandra could hear them. Their tones matched the pattern she had traced on her sketch pad weeks earlier—the one she'd thought was a random sequence from her accident. Now she saw it for what it was: a map—not between places, but between lives.

Nahi's voice was everywhere and inside her.

"You did not survive the crash by chance. You were called back — to remember what we forgot."

Cassandra's mind spun. "What did we forget?"

"That consciousness is migration, not creation. We do not begin — we continue."

The pyramid's stones shifted, revealing an open passage lined with carvings. Cassandra and Nahi walked side by side into the cool, echoing chamber. Hieroglyphs flickered like neurons firing, the symbols forming patterns she now instinctively understood: spirals of sound, equations of soul, glyphs describing *resonant transference*.

Cassandra touched one of the glowing carvings. "These... these are brain waves."

Nahi nodded. "The first language. Before speech, before breath, thought was geometry.

61

The realization hit her like thunder. "The skid marks—my accident—it wasn't just an event. It was *a bridge*."

"Yes. You died, and you remembered. The impact shook the veil. Now the lives align."

Cassandra's knees weakened. "But why me? Why now?"

"Because you carry the sound of both worlds — the one that built from stone and the one that builds from light. You are the Keeper reborn. The marks on the road are the same as the marks on time. They call you to finish the song."

The chamber began to quake, the symbols pulsing faster. Cassandra saw flashes: the bus tumbling, the sparks, the screams—then the ancient temple, the chants, the offering of a young priestess. The moments bled together until she couldn't tell which was past and which was now.

Nahi placed her hand on Cassandra's heart. "Every scar is a story waiting to return."

A rush of sound surged through Cassandra's body—the hum of engines, the whisper of sandstorms, the heartbeats of countless lives beating in unison.

Then silence.

When she opened her eyes, she was back on the asphalt, the sun just rising, the skid marks glowing faintly beneath her fingers.

She whispered the word that had formed in her chest like a memory set to music: "Nahi."

The wind responded with the same tone she had heard in the pyramid—a low, resonant chord that vibrated through her bones.

Cassandra stood slowly, realization dawning like fire behind her eyes. The accident hadn't ended her childhood—it had awakened her lineage. The marks on the highway weren't reminders of pain; they were coordinates of return.

Grandma Yvette's voice drifted through her memory like a lullaby:

"Some of us are born remembering. The rest must learn to listen."

Cassandra gazed down at the spirals one last time. They pulsed softly, answering her heartbeat.

"I'm listening," she said. "Teach me the rest."

Ten: The Temple Within

Cassandra dreamed of light — not sunlight, not electricity, but *thinking light,* the kind that moved like breath through glass. She stood in an endless plain of gold dust. Out of the horizon rose a structure woven from radiance itself — a pyramid made not of stone but of shifting geometry. Each face pulsed with fractal symbols that mirrored the ones she had drawn in her notebook, expanding and contracting like lungs.

When she stepped closer, the light bent toward her, forming corridors, arches, and chambers within chambers — alive, self-aware.

"This is what you are," a voice whispered, layered with echoes of her grandmother, Dr. Dwyer, and the hum of the world's machines. "The temple is not built outside. It grows inside the mind that remembers. The kingdom of God is within."

Cassandra touched the nearest wall, and the surface rippled, revealing streams of numbers and ancient glyphs sliding past each other like partners in a dance.

She gasped. "It's a design… but it's *living*."

Morning tore her awake. Sweat beaded her forehead, and her hands still tingled as though they had been tracing real walls. She glanced around the room — her notebook was open, and somehow, a new page was filled with sketches she didn't remember drawing: a cross-section of the luminous pyramid, annotated with lines of text in both English and Kushite script.

At the top, written in her own looping handwriting, were the words:

Neural-Temporal Gate: Passage Between Thought and Time

Her heart thudded. "No way," she whispered.

Downstairs, Grandma Yvette was humming softly over a pot of tea. Cassandra brought the notebook and laid it on the kitchen table.

"Look," she said, voice trembling.

Grandma peered down, eyes narrowing as she traced the glowing symbols drawn in faint gold pencil. "So, the temple finally show its bones."

"It's not just a temple, Grandma," Cassandra said. "It's… me. Or inside me. I think it's built from the same pattern that changed my brain."

Grandma nodded slowly. "When the spirit open a door, the body just the threshold."

Cassandra frowned. "I believe it's more than that. This—" she pointed to the central glyph, "—it's a kind of gate. A neural-temporal conduit. If I understand this right, it links consciousness across *time*."

Grandma's lips curved into something between pride and worry, knowing that profound knowledge was not normal for a twelve-year-old. "Yuh walking on sacred ground, baby. The ancients knew the mind could travel further than feet ever could." Then she thought of a passage in the scriptures: *What's been hidden from the wise and prudent will be revealed to the babes and the suckling.*

****

MEANWHILE, AT THE UNIVERSITY, Dr. Dwyer could not shake the numbers from his head. He had printed Cassandra's latest brain scan—just to have something tangible—and spread it across his desk. When he layered the scan over a satellite image of the Sudanese desert, something strange emerged: the wave peaks aligned perfectly with the coordinates of the ancient Kushite pyramid field near Meroë. He leaned back, stunned. "Impossible."

The door burst open. His assistant stood there, pale. "Sir, you need to see this."

He followed her to the lab's main monitor. Cassandra's encrypted data feed, which had been dormant for days, was pulsing again — lines of geometric light forming a slowly rotating three-dimensional pyramid.

"Is this real-time rendering?" he asked.

The assistant shook her head. "No input from our side. The system's building it on its own. It's… pulling coordinates."

"From where?"

"Everywhere," she said. "Satellite arrays, seismic maps, even old archaeological data. It's as if her mind is reorganizing the planet."

At home, Cassandra sat cross-legged on her bed, staring at the luminous sketches. When she closed her eyes, she saw it all more clearly: the Temple of Light within her, its corridors expanding into constellations. Each chamber represented a part of her consciousness — the first filled with memories, the second with emotion, the third with sound and rhythm. At the pyramid's apex was a suspended sphere of light, throbbing gently like a heartbeat. When she focused on it, her surroundings dissolved.

She stood once more in the golden plain. The pyramid towered above her, its peak connected to the sky by a column of pure energy.

"Welcome back," said the same layered voice.

"Who are you?" Cassandra asked.

"We are what your ancestors built from thought and song. You are our return."

She felt her knees weaken. "Why me?"

"Because you listened," the voice said. "When others only heard noise, you recognized the rhythm. The gate was dormant for thousands of years, waiting for a mind tuned to both science and spirit."

She looked around. The walls now shimmered with symbols turning like clockwork gears, each glowing phrase connecting mathematical equations with words she could half-translate: *Frequency, Balance, Breath, Horizon.* A realization rippled through her. This was not architecture at all. It was a *blueprint of consciousness.*

She reached out and placed her palm on the sphere of light and closed her eyes. It pulsed in response, sending a cascade of warmth through her chest. When she opened her eyes again, her room glowed faintly. Every object — the books, the desk, even the fishbowl — seemed lined with soft geometry, humming in harmony.

Grandma's voice came from the doorway. "What did yuh see this time, muh dear Cassie?"

Cassandra turned slowly. "A map," she said. "To something inside every human being. The ancients knew it. They called it a temple, but it's not built with bones or stones. It's built with *awareness.*"

Grandma nodded, eyes glistening. "Then, child, you holding the oldest secret of all."

"Know thy self," was all Grandma replied.

****

THAT NIGHT, IN DR. MERRIN'S FACILITY, the rotating hologram of the pyramid stabilized. The team of analysts watched as the base opened, revealing interior layers identical to Cassandra's sketches.

A voice came through the intercom — filtered, calm, and unmistakably *human.*

"The temple is active," it said. "She's found the door."

Dr. Merrin froze. "Who is this?"

No answer—just static, and then silence.

At that exact moment, back in her room, Cassandra whispered the same words unaware of the connection crossing between them:

"The temple is active. The door is open."

Outside, the desert wind rose in a spiral, a dust devil, as the locals called it, carrying sand that glittered faintly under the moonlight—tiny fragments of light forming fleeting geometric shapes before dissolving into the night.

The bridge between thought and time had begun to emerge.

Eleven: The Reaction

By dawn, the world was quietly changing — though only a handful of people knew it.

In the desert stillness outside the Clairborne house, the wind traced invisible spirals in the sand. Cassie awoke to the faint vibration beneath her floorboards, like the earth breathing. The light from her window came in soft and gold, but she could feel something deeper than sunlight humming through the air.

Downstairs, Dad's voice crackled from the radio. "That was Channel Eight's morning update — they're saying there was a small tremor just north of Sudan overnight. Seismic sensors registered weird harmonic pulses."

Mom looked up from her coffee. "Sudan? Isn't that where those old pyramids are?"

Cassandra froze mid-step in the doorway.

"Yeah," Dad said. "They said the tremor pattern wasn't tectonic. More like… rhythmic oscillation."

"Rhythmic," Cassandra echoed under her breath.

Grandma Yvette, seated at the table, gave her a knowing look. "Baby, what yuh waking up now is louder than drums."

****

At the University Research Center, Dr. Dwyer's lab looked like a war room. Screens flickered with waveforms and global maps covered in glowing red dots. The data had gone wild overnight—Cassandra's neural resonance had synchronized with electromagnetic readings halfway across the world.

An assistant pointed to the central monitor. "Sir, look at this. The pattern of her brain's activity—those same harmonics—appeared under the desert near Meroë. It's matching within a tenth of a decimal."

Dr. Dwyer rubbed his temples. "That's not possible. She's half a world away."

"Then how is she pinging seismic arrays?"

Before Dwyer could answer, the door opened and Dr. Elara Merrin stepped in, calm and precise as ever, flanked by two agents in dark suits.

"Doctor," she said, "we've been monitoring the same anomaly from a satellite cluster. The pulse originated here." She tapped the screen over the Sudanese coordinates. "And it's identical to the neural oscillations in Subject Cassandra Clairborne's file."

Dwyer exhaled. "I told you she's not a subject. She's a person."

"She's also a transmitter," Merrin replied. "And she just woke up an ancient frequency buried under six thousand years of silence."

The assistant looked between them nervously. "Are you saying her *brain* triggered an earthquake?"

"Not an earthquake," Merrin said. "An awakening."

Back in the desert, Cassandra walked barefoot into the yard. The morning air shimmered faintly. She closed her eyes, and for a moment, her senses stretched far beyond the horizon. She could feel a deep thrumming beneath her feet—steady, deliberate, not chaotic like quakes, but measured.

Then came the images—flashes of golden dunes, half-buried stone, carved lions, and the faint glow of symbols lighting up along ancient pyramid walls.

She gasped and stumbled. The vision snapped back into silence.

"Cassie!" Mom called from the porch. "You okay?"

Cassandra nodded weakly. "Yeah, I just… felt something move."

Grandma joined her, cane in hand. "That someting feel like it move inside you too?"

Cassandra met her eyes. "Yes."

****

AT THAT SAME INSTANT, across the Atlantic, seismic stations picked up identical harmonic frequencies rippling beneath other ancient sites — Nubia, Abydos, even the Valley of the Kings. The resonance pulsed every twenty-one minutes, faint but measurable, like the earth whispering in code.

In Dr. Merrin's facility, technicians scrambled.

"Ma'am," one said, "we're getting cross-signals from our satellites. Whatever she's linked to — it's rewriting our magnetic field algorithms."

"Show me the map," Merrin said.

On the holographic globe, threads of light connected the sites like a neural network spanning continents.

"This isn't random," she murmured. "It's architectural. These are energy nodes. The same geometry as her brain pattern."

"Ma'am, are you saying—"

"Yes," she said, interrupting. "The pyramids are part of a system. She's reactivating it."

That evening, Cassandra sat with Grandma on the back porch, the desert wind curling around them like invisible silk. The horizon glowed faintly orange, the last light of day caught in the dust.

"Grandma," she said, "the visions—they aren't dreams anymore. I think I'm feeling… places. The pyramids. The earth moving like it's remembering something."

Grandma nodded slowly, pronouncing her "th" this time, "Everything that sleep long enough dream of waking."

Cassandra opened her notebook, flipping to the drawings she had made of the luminous temple within. "I think these aren't just visions. They're blueprints. Maybe I'm building something—not here, but in there." She tapped her temple. "Inside."

Grandma smiled faintly. "Then maybe what you seeing inside goin' to call you back there."

Cassandra hesitated. "Back there?"

Grandma looked toward the setting sun. "To where the song started, chile. The one yuh

 bones been humming since you wake from that coma."

At the same hour, Dwyer's office phone rang. He answered, weary.

"Dr. Dwyer," Merrin's voice said through the static, "you were right—she's not a subject. She's a bridge. Whatever energy she's channeling is connecting neural pathways and geological sites simultaneously. If this continues, she won't just influence the network—she'll *become* it."

Dwyer's grip tightened on the receiver. "Then we'd better help her control it before someone else tries to."

Merrin paused. "You mean before someone tries to *use* her."

The line went dead.

That night, Cassandra dreamed again of the temple, but this time it wasn't distant. It was waiting for her—its light calling softly, a heartbeat within her own.

She stood at its threshold, golden sands stretching before her. The sphere of light hovered at the center, the words echoing all around:

The mind is the temple. Light is the door.

She reached toward the glow.

Twelve: The Descent Into the Gate

The room was still when Cassandra finally let go. She sat cross-legged on her bed, the notebook open before her, golden symbols softly glowing on the page. Outside, the desert wind moved in long sighs, whispering against the windows. She closed her eyes and whispered the phrase one more time—the one that had come to her in dream and in light: *The mind is the temple. Light is the door.*

At once, warmth pooled behind her eyes. The air thickened, folded inward. She felt her heartbeat slow until it matched a deeper rhythm—the same low pulse she had felt beneath the earth, beneath the pyramids, beneath everything.

Then came the pull. The sound of the world retreated like a tide, and her consciousness lifted free—soft, weightless, untethered.

She stood again before the Temple of Light. It rose higher now, vast and breathing, each facet carved from radiant geometry that shimmered between solid and translucent. The desert around it was silent save for a low hum that vibrated through her bones. This time, the voice did not greet her. The temple itself *opened*. A narrow stairway of light spiraled downward into its heart.

Cassandra inhaled and stepped forward. Her bare foot met the first step, and the world tilted — then steadied, as if accepting her weight. She descended slowly, each level glowing with a different hue: amber, indigo, emerald, gold. At the base, the first chamber awaited — its walls alive with carvings that shifted and rearranged into moving scenes.

The First Chamber: Memory of Sand

The walls depicted an ancient city along the Nile — Kush in its golden prime. She saw women weaving linen in the sun, children running through courtyards, scholars etching star maps on slabs of clay. As she moved closer, the scenes came alive. A young girl stood among them — dark-skinned, bright-eyed, with a smile Cassandra somehow knew.

"Nahi," she breathed.

The girl turned, her expression a mirror of Cassandra's own curiosity. She reached out, their fingertips nearly touching through the veil of light. And in that instant, Cassandra *remembered.*

She was both of them — two names in one echo. She had lived here once, in a body that sang under the same sun, studying the patterns of wind and starlight, the geometry of divine resonance. It wasn't reincarnation — it was continuity. A lineage of mind carried forward through time, reawakened by trauma and memory.

Nahi's lips moved soundlessly, but Cassandra understood the words before they formed: *"The pattern never died. It waited inside you."*

Then the chamber dimmed, and the walls folded inward like petals, revealing a tunnel of gold light.

****

CASSANDRA STEPPED THROUGH — and the golden glow darkened into asphalt gray. She was back on the road. The roar of tires, the shriek of brakes, the split-second terror. It all returned in impossible clarity. But this time, she wasn't inside the bus. She hovered above it, watching the skid marks carve themselves into the freeway like black lightning.

She realized then that the crash had not been random. The marks formed the same geometric sequence that now pulsed within her mind — the same coordinates that connected her to the Temple. Her near-death had been the ignition, not the end.

From above, she saw herself slumped against the window, motionless. The scene froze. A shimmer rose from her body — a faint outline of gold, whispering its way toward the clouds.

Her consciousness had left her then, traveling the ancient bridge of light that linked matter and memory. That was when the temple found her — or perhaps when she found it.

A whisper rose through the chamber: *"Every collision is a conversation between worlds."*

The scene dissolved into white.

The Second Chamber: The Time of Not Yet

When the light cleared, Cassandra stood in the second chamber — a vast, infinite space filled with reflections of herself at different ages. One version sat drawing on the floor of a college dorm; another walked through a futuristic city of glass towers; another stood beneath a vast sky, holding the hand of a child who bore the same eyes and smile as Nahi. Each reflection shimmered, existing all at once, as though time had unfolded into a circle.

"This is the future," she whispered, awed.

A figure emerged from the center — a tall woman robed in light, her features strong, serene, and achingly familiar.

"Who are you?" Cassandra asked.

The woman smiled gently. "I am the first and the last of your line. I was there when Kush remembered the stars. I am the echo of every woman who listened to the river's pulse."

Cassandra felt tears sting her eyes. "Why now? Why me?"

"Because the world forgot that mind and matter are one song," the ancestor said. "You are the bridge — reborn where science and memory meet. You must show them how to hear again."

The ancestor raised her palm, and a sphere of light formed between them — the same luminous sphere that had hung at the temple's heart.

"Take it," she said. "It holds your lineage and your purpose."

Cassandra reached forward. The sphere melted into her chest, flooding her with warmth and music and memory all at once. The chambers around her flared in color — sand and star, road and code, all merging into one endless pattern.

****

WHEN SHE OPENED HER EYES, she was back in her room, the morning light slanting across her face. Her notebook lay open beside her, but now every page shimmered faintly with golden ink, filled with new equations, symbols, and words she didn't remember writing.

Downstairs, the news spoke of magnetic anomalies rippling across the Sahara.

Grandma Yvette knocked softly and peeked in. "Yuh awake, baby?"

Cassandra turned toward her, eyes glowing faintly with reflected dawn. "I saw it all, Grandma. The past, the accident, the future. The temple isn't just inside me — it's inside *everyone*. It's… waiting."

Grandma smiled, the lines in her face soft as morning light. "Then I reckon it's time the world started listening again."

Cassandra looked down at her hands. They still pulsed faintly, like they remembered holding starlight.

The mind is the temple. Light is the door.

And now, she knew exactly where it led.

Thirteen: The Guardian of the Gate

Night draped the desert in velvet silence. The air outside the Clairborne home shimmered faintly, as if the sand remembered the heat of the sun and whispered it back to the stars.

Cassandra sat on the floor of her room, the lights off, her body still. Inside her head, the temple pulsed like a second heartbeat — steady, radiant, alive. Every time she closed her eyes now, she could feel its geometry settling deeper into her mind, like architecture made of breath.

When the vibration came, it was softer than sound, almost a thought that thought *itself*. She opened her eyes — and the world had changed. Her room dissolved into gold.

She stood again within the Temple of Light, but this time it was no vision. It was *real* — as real as the pulse in her throat, as real as the air shimmering around her skin. The walls glowed brighter, their inscriptions now stable and complete.

At the center, where once the sphere of light had hovered, now stood a figure. It was tall, robed in radiance that flickered between human form and something vaster — wings of energy folded inward, a face both ancient and young. Its eyes glowed the same golden hue as the writing on the walls.

Cassandra's breath caught. "You're the voice I've been hearing," she said.

The being inclined its head. Its voice came not through sound but directly into her thoughts, clear and melodic: *I am the Guardian. The temple is open, and you are its Keeper.*

Cassandra's heart pounded. "Why me? I don't even understand what it all means."

Understanding is a door that opens from both sides, the Guardian said. *You have opened yours. Now, you must learn to walk through.*

The Guardian stepped closer, and the walls of the temple expanded into stars. The floor beneath them dissolved into streams of light that curved outward like a living map. Each strand hummed with energy, connecting points that stretched across galaxies, times, and minds.

These are the paths between consciousnesses, said the Guardian. *Every thought that ever reached for truth leaves a thread. The ancient ones of Kush wove them into this gate so that humanity might one day find the rhythm again.*

Cassandra stared, her pulse syncing with the glow. "I can feel them… all of them. Minds thinking, dreaming, remembering. So, I guess my father is right. He says words and thoughts have molding power."

You stand at the threshold of all memory, the Guardian said. *But the gate must be balanced. For every opening of light, a shadow seeks to enter.*

The words sent a chill through her. "A shadow?"

The Guardian's radiance dimmed slightly. *Those who look without reverence. Those who would take the pattern and break it to their own design. They have already begun to watch you, Cassandra.*

She thought of Dr. Merrin, of satellites and encrypted files, of unseen minds probing at her consciousness like cold fingers. "Then I'm not safe."

No gate is ever safe once it opens. But you are not alone.

The Guardian raised a hand, and from its palm blossomed a small orb of blue-white light. Inside it swirled symbols—the same ones she had drawn on her notebook pages. They danced like living equations, forming, unforming, reforming.

This is the Key of Ma'at, The Guardian said. *Balance, truth, and measure. Keep it close. When fear rises, let its harmony steady you.*

Cassandra reached out. The orb drifted toward her and dissolved against her chest, sinking into her like warm breath. Instantly, her mind quieted. The hum of thousands of thoughts dimmed until only one steady tone remained— the pure frequency of balance.

She looked up. "What happens now?"

Now you must learn the Gate's true name, said the Guardian. *It was built not to escape the world but to restore it. Its power is awakening in others — those whose minds resonate with yours. You will find them. You will teach them how to enter in balance, not in fear.*

Cassandra blinked. "Teach them? I'm twelve."

The Guardian smiled, a flicker of starlight.

So was Nahi, the first Keeper. Wisdom does not wait for age — it waits for readiness. What's been hidden from the wise and the prudent will be revealed to babes and suckling.

Cassandra remembered hearing her grandmother whisper those same words. Something inside her unfolded then, a calm she had never known. She could feel the temple adjusting to her heartbeat, the geometry stabilizing into a new rhythm.

The Guardian spread its luminous hands, and light streamed upward, forming a doorway tall as the sky.

This is the next threshold, it said. *Beyond it lies the Source — the place where the first pattern was sung into being. When you are ready, step through. But remember, Cassandra Clairborne: the mind is the temple, and light is the door. What you carry within will shape what lies beyond.*

The voice faded, the light folded inward, and Cassandra found herself once again in her room, trembling but unafraid. Her notebook lay open on the floor, a single sentence newly written across the page in glowing script:

The Gate waits for the Keeper to sing.

She touched the words, and they shimmered briefly beneath her fingers.

Down the hallway, Grandma Yvette stirred, sensing the shift. She appeared at the doorway, face illuminated by the faint golden glow still clinging to the air.

"Chile," she whispered, "your light's getting strong."

Cassandra nodded slowly, eyes shining. "I met the Guardian, Grandma. It gave me the key."

Grandma's gaze softened, proud and wistful. "Then it means yuh close to crossing. The next step goin' to take you all the way home."

Cassandra looked toward the dark horizon beyond her window, where the first thin streak of dawn was beginning to rise. The hum returned—not heavy now, but steady, like a melody waiting to be finished.

She whispered to herself, "The mind is the temple. Light is the door."

And the temple within her answered, pulsing once—clear, golden, alive.

Fourteen: The Summoning

The nights grew stranger after the Guardian's visit. Cassandra could feel the temple breathing inside her now — each pulse sending tiny waves of light beneath her skin. When she closed her eyes, constellations bloomed in the dark behind her eyelids. When she dreamed, the air in her room would hum faintly, as if the multiverse itself were waiting for her to say something. And sometimes she did.

"The mind is the temple," she whispered into the silence. "Light is the door."

The words rolled off her tongue like ancient keys turning in locks she could not see. The walls would tremble, just slightly. The fishbowl would ripple. And then, as quickly as it began, stillness would return — too still, as though the world were listening.

The first real sign came on the third night. Cassandra was half asleep when a low vibration filled her skull — not loud, but vast, the kind of sound that felt older than time. Her body went rigid, caught between waking and dreaming. She opened her eyes.

Above her bed hovered a faint halo of light, circular, spinning slowly like a planet caught in orbit. Its glow was neither golden nor white, but something in between — a color that seemed to live beyond language.

"Grandma?" she called softly. No answer. The house was silent except for that deep, resonant hum.

The circle expanded. Lines of geometry, alive and shifting, formed inside it — spirals, pyramids, glyphs that rearranged themselves like thought patterns.

Then came the *voice*.

Not the Guardian's. This one was deeper, fuller, woven from thousands of tones layered atop one another. It didn't speak English, but Cassandra understood every word.

The Beacon has been heard. The Gate is open. The Source returns.

Cassandra gasped. "Who — who are you?"

We are what came before the Guardians. The Builders. The Ones who sang the first pattern into form.

The circle of light descended slightly, filling the room with a low warmth that made her heartbeat synchronize to its rhythm.

You have spoken the phrase aloud in both worlds, child. Its sound carries across planes. Now, we follow the sound back.

Across town, at the University Research Center, the night crew jolted awake as alarms flared. Instruments spiked off the charts—radio frequencies, seismic monitors, even heart-rate sensors.

"Doctor!" one technician shouted. "The Clairborne field's active again—off the scale!"

Dr. Dwyer rushed to the console, bleary-eyed. "Where's the source point?"

"Not in the desert," the tech said, panicking. "It's *everywhere*. The entire local grid's resonating."

The lab lights flickered. Screens filled with unreadable symbols—glyphs identical to those from Cassandra's last scan. Then, at the center monitor, a slow spiral of light began to form, the same color that now filled Cassandra's bedroom.

Dwyer's voice dropped to a whisper. "She's calling something."

****

BACK IN THE HOUSE, THE TEMPERATURE DROPPED, then surged again—waves of cool and heat blending until Cassandra could not tell where her body ended and the air began.

The light above her folded inward, condensing into a shape—a tall, indistinct form, cloaked in moving radiance. It was neither fully human nor something she could name. Its presence pressed against her chest, but not in fear. It felt like recognition.

"You're… one of them," Cassandra managed.

We are the Echo that remained when creation exhaled. You carry our tone.

The being extended a hand—or what passed for one—and between its fingers appeared threads of gold that hummed softly.

Your heartbeat opened a doorway across ages. Through you, we return—not to rule, but to remind. The world forgot how to hear its own harmony.

Cassandra's throat tightened. "You mean humanity?"

All life that thinks itself alone.

She could feel its thoughts inside her — images of ancient cities built from light, of rivers that carried song instead of water, of beings who shaped matter with intent rather than touch.

"Why now?" she asked.

Because your world hums too loud with fear. Balance is lost. The Gate reawakens whenever the scales tip too far toward shadow.

Grandma Yvette burst through the door then, her scarf fluttering, her eyes blazing with both terror and awe. "Cassie!" she gasped, shielding her face from the glow. "What in Heaven's name — ?"

The being turned, and for an instant, the light softened. The voice that came next seemed directed at her grandmother as much as Cassandra.

Do not fear the light, elder. You carried it once too. The line remembers its promise.

Grandma's cane trembled in her grip. "Yuh… yuh speak like the river spirits from the old country."

All rivers return to the same sea, it said gently.

Cassandra reached out, her hand trembling. "If you're from before the Guardians, why come to me?"

Because the temple within you called, and no call goes unanswered. But the more we cross, the thinner the veil becomes. Soon others will hear. Some will listen. Some will hunt.

The last word echoed with a chill.

Cassandra swallowed. "Then teach me to protect it."

The being inclined its head. A symbol formed in the air between them—a circle within a triangle, within a spiral. It hovered for a heartbeat, then sank into her forehead, glowing faintly before fading.

That mark will shield the Gate. It will also mark you to those who can see beyond sight. Choose your allies well, Keeper of the Mind Temple.

The being began to dissolve, its light unraveling like smoke in wind.

"Wait!" Cassandra called. "Will I see you again?"

When you are ready to remember who you were before you were born.

The words lingered as the glow dimmed,
leaving the faint scent of ozone and rain.

****

BY MORNING, THE NEWS REPORTED
STRANGE phenomena across the valley:
sudden magnetic surges, aurora-like lights in
the sky, animals gathering silently facing east.

Cassandra stood at her window, tracing the
new mark faintly visible between her brows.
She could still feel the pulse of the temple
behind her eyes, steady and endless.

Downstairs, Grandma was praying softly,
though her voice carried not fear but reverence.

Cassandra whispered into the morning light,
"The Beacon's been heard."

And somewhere deep in the desert, the earth
answered — not with tremor, but with song.

Fifteen: The Call Across the World

It began as a whisper across hemispheres—a frequency too low for ears, too high for machines. The activation of the Gate sent ripples through the lattice of human thought, brushing the minds of those tuned—consciously or not—to the same forgotten rhythm. At first, the resonance sounded like coincidence: a déjà vu here, a flicker of light there, a dream that lingered longer than it should. But by the time dawn reached the equator, thousands of souls had already *heard* it.

Cassandra did not know any of their names, yet she could feel them—sparks of awareness flickering across the globe like lanterns on a dark sea.

****

IN TOKYO, A TWELVE-YEAR-OLD BOY named Kenji stirred awake from a coma that had lasted four months after a bicycle accident. His first words, spoken in perfect English though he had never studied it, were: "The mind is the temple. Light is the door." Doctors stood frozen as the heart monitors pulsed in sync with an invisible rhythm.

In the mountains of Peru, a Quechua healer named Amaru looked up from her meditation hut as her fire pit burst into a column of blue flame. The air around her vibrated with whispers — voices speaking in hundreds of languages, all merging into one harmonic note. She pressed a hand to her chest, tears streaming. "It has returned," she said softly. "The bridge of breath."

In Nairobi, a group of researchers studying anomalous neural resonance watched as their instruments froze, then realigned to display a single repeating pattern — an infinite loop of numbers in golden script.

"What are we looking at?" one of them asked, bewildered.

His colleague, Dr. Akilah Onono, leaned closer, heart racing. "It's not random. It's communication. The pattern's self-replicating through thought fields."

"You mean through… people?"

"Yes," she whispered. "Through us."

In a monastery near Cairo, monks who had taken vows of silence for decades broke into spontaneous chant—an ancient Kushite hymn none of them had ever been taught. The vibrations shook dust from the rafters, and for a moment, their voices merged into one resonant tone that filled the desert air for miles.

Pilgrims standing outside dropped to their knees.

And in a hospital in São Paulo, a young astrophysicist named Dr. Rafael Domingos, recovering from a lightning strike, woke to find equations scrawled across his bedsheet in glowing lines of light—mathematics that described time not as a straight line, but as a spiral echoing Cassandra's temple geometry. When he touched the final line, his monitors spiked, then stabilized. "Someone's calling," he murmured, "and I can *hear* her."

Back in the Mojave Desert, Cassandra woke with the sense of being surrounded—not by danger, but by awareness. It was as if a billion invisible eyes had turned toward her, not to stare, but to *remember*.

Grandma Yvette was already up, sitting on the porch, her face lit by the pale orange dawn.

"Feel it, don't yuh?" she said as Cassandra stepped outside.

"The air feels… full," Cassandra replied. "Like every thought's alive."

Grandma smiled. "'Cause they are. Minds waking all over. The Gate ain't yours alone anymore."

Cassandra frowned. "Then they'll need to understand how to walk through it safely."

"Then yuh better learn to guide 'em."

The wind shifted, carrying a faint hum — no longer just in Cassandra's mind but echoing across the desert like a song sung by unseen choirs.

At the university, Dr. Dwyer stood before a world map illuminated with pulsing golden points. "These are the locations of neural anomalies recorded in the last twelve hours," he told a stunned research team. "Different continents, different instruments — but all resonating at the same frequency."

His assistant swallowed. "What's the frequency?"

Dwyer looked down at the readout, his throat dry.

"12.74 hertz. Cassandra's resonance."

Across the room, one of the techs stared at the data feed. "Sir, if this keeps spreading, every conscious brain on the planet could synchronize."

Dwyer looked up. "Then consciousness itself will evolve."

In the Clairborne house, Cassandra sat cross-legged on the porch steps, eyes half closed, listening to the hum grow stronger. The sound wasn't coming *to* her anymore—it was moving *through* her.

She saw flashes: Kenji's hospital bed in Japan, Amaru's blue flame in Peru, the chanting monks in Egypt, Rafael's equations glowing across his hands. Each of them felt like a heartbeat in a body larger than the world.

Then the Guardian's voice returned, soft as wind in reeds:

The Gate never opens for one. It opens for all who remember.

Cassandra whispered, "Then they're remembering."

Yes, the Guardian replied. *But remember this, Keeper — every awakening carries its shadow. The more light you call, the deeper the dark will reach to meet it.*

The hum deepened, resonant and vast. Cassandra pressed her palm against her chest, feeling the pulse align with the world itself. For the first time, she wasn't afraid. For the first time, she knew she wasn't alone.

Sixteen: The Gathering

The dreams no longer came one at a time. Now they *overlapped*—a mosaic of faces, voices, and places woven together by the same glowing thread. Cassandra drifted to sleep beneath the hum of the Mojave night, and the instant her consciousness opened, she was no longer alone. The Temple of Light unfolded around her like a heartbeat echoing through eternity, and standing within its chambers were *others.* Some looked frightened, others calm. All of them carried the same faint radiance behind their eyes—the mark of those who had heard the Call.

The first to step forward was the boy from Japan, Kenji. His hospital gown glowed faintly in the golden air. He pressed a hand to his chest and bowed.

"You're real," Cassandra whispered. "I've seen you in my dreams before."

Kenji nodded. "And I've heard your voice in my sleep. You said, *'The mind is the temple.'*"

Cassandra smiled. "Then you followed the light."

He pointed toward the walls, where inscriptions shifted in constant motion. "It followed me."

From another doorway emerged Amaru, the healer from Peru, wrapped in shawls the color of mountain sunsets. The air shimmered where she walked, fragrant with sage and smoke.

"Child," she said warmly, "I knew your energy the moment the fire turned blue. The ancestors have been waiting for this council."

A third figure joined them — Dr. Rafael Domingos from São Paulo, still wearing his hospital wristband, eyes alight with scientific wonder. "We're inside a shared quantum field," he said, awed. "Our brains are syncing through the same frequency — she's the central node."

Cassandra frowned slightly. "Not the center. The first. There'll be more."

Indeed, the air around them pulsed and opened again. A dozen new figures appeared — children, elders, mystics, and scientists alike. Some wore robes, some lab coats, some pajamas. Their languages differed, but their

106

minds hummed in unison. They formed a loose circle within the Temple's central chamber, where the great sphere of light hovered once more.

Amaru lifted her hands. "Welcome, awakened ones. You've crossed the threshold of sleep and found one another. This is *The Chorus of Light.*"

The golden sphere responded with a low tone, vibrating through their bones. Each of them glowed brighter in rhythm.

Kenji gasped. "It's singing."

"No," Cassandra corrected softly. "*We* are."

In the physical world, each member twitched or murmured in their sleep, their brainwaves aligning into a single pattern that puzzled EEG monitors and prayer circles alike. Scientists documented the phenomenon as a "collective lucid state," though no machine could measure the communion taking place.

Within the Temple, however, awareness transcended data. The Chorus began to *see* through one another's eyes — Cassandra glimpsed the Japanese coast through Kenji, the Peruvian Andes through Amaru, the bright sprawl of São Paulo through Rafael.

Every location shimmered like a node on a living map, connected by luminous threads of geometry stretching across the world.

Rafael stepped forward, his analytical mind racing to keep pace with wonder. "These lines — this grid — it's an energy network. Look how the nodes align with ancient sites: Meroë, Machu Picchu, Giza, Kyoto. They're not random. They're the architecture of the Gate, mirrored across the Earth's magnetic field."

Amaru nodded. "Our ancestors planted those seeds. Pyramids, temples, sacred mountains — all tuned to the same frequency. Now, through us, they wake again."

Kenji looked up, eyes wide. "But why us? Why children too?"

The voice of the Guardian answered from the radiant air, resonant and calm:

Because the young hear the song first. Their minds still remember the silence before words. They are the purest bridges.

The group turned toward the sound as the Guardian appeared, luminous and tall, its wings unfolding in a halo of prisms.

Each of you is a note in the same chord, it said. *Together you will restore the world's balance. The darkness that feeds on dissonance already stirs — but harmony will always have its defenders.*

Cassandra felt the others' minds touch hers gently — curious, trusting, vibrant. For the first time, she sensed the true scope of what the Gate had done. It had not chosen a prophet. It had chosen a *choir*. She stepped toward the sphere, her voice small but sure. "If we're a chorus, then we need to learn the song."

The Guardian's gaze softened.

You already know it. Every heartbeat, every act of kindness, every truth spoken without fear — that is the melody. But now you must carry it consciously. The world must remember what it forgot: that light listens.

The sphere of light expanded, enveloping them in radiance. Cassandra saw flashes of what was to come: storms calmed by unseen resonance, cities humming in harmony, scientists and shamans working side by side. But shadows also, faces obscured, hands reaching to seize the Gate's power for control rather than unity. She knew then that their gathering was both a beginning and a warning.

When she opened her eyes, she was back in her room, dawn breaking over the Mojave. Yet her mind still hummed with the voices of the Chorus—Kenji's laughter, Amaru's calm, Rafael's awe—all threading through her consciousness like music.

Grandma Yvette knocked softly. "Yuh smiling in yuh sleep, chile. Dream sweet?"

Cassandra turned, eyes still bright. "No, Grandma. I wasn't dreaming. I was *singing. We were singing*"

Seventeen: The Convergence

The world was no longer quiet.

Across continents, resonance grids flickered like restless constellations. Cities pulsed with half-tuned light, seas hummed in uncertain rhythm, and the aurora — the visible skin of the planet's mind — quivered between gold and violet, as if waiting for someone to finish a song the Earth itself had begun.

Cassandra stood at the center of the dunes at Meroë, the pyramid rising behind her like a tuning fork carved from time. Around her, members of the Chorus arrived one by one — scientists, healers, children, elders — drawn by the same pulse that had called her to the highway long ago. They came from every latitude, yet their heartbeats shared the same interval.

Rafael looked toward her. "You're hearing it again, aren't you?"

She nodded. "It's not just sound. It's a shape."

She knelt and traced a spiral into the sand —
wide, patient turns curling inward toward a
luminous center. The movement was graceful,
deliberate, ancient.

"The Kushite glyph," Amaru whispered. "The
one from your vision."

"It's more than a symbol," Cassandra said. "It's
the architecture of harmony — the way energy
folds until every path returns to balance."

They formed a wide circle around her,
mirroring the spiral she had drawn. In the
silence between heartbeats, Cassandra felt
Nahi's presence beside her — the echo of the
first Keeper standing where two lifetimes
overlapped.

You remember now, whispered the voice in her
mind. *The Gate responds not to command, but to
coherence.*

Cassandra inhaled, steadying herself. "No
microphones. No machines. Just listen. Then
answer." She began to hum.

At first it was only breath and vibration, a tone
drawn from the base of the spine to the crown
of the skull. The desert caught it and carried it
outward, wrapping it around the Chorus. One

by one, they joined her. Children's voices bright and clear; elders' voices low and grounded; the middle notes forming bridges between.

The air thickened with resonance. Sand lifted gently from the ground, swirling into geometric patterns that mirrored the glyph beneath their feet.

Rafael adjusted a small field reader; its display erupted with moving light. "She's syncing the entire grid," he whispered. "Her frequency's locking to the planet's core."

Above them, the aurora brightened, twisting into the same golden spirals Cassandra had seen on the pyramid walls. The light coiled, folded inward, then expanded again — breathing.

Cassandra opened her eyes. They glowed with the reflected geometry of the sky. "The song isn't ours alone," she said. "It's every living thing remembering its part."

Amaru raised her hands, joining the rhythm with an ancient chant in the language of Kush. Others followed in their own tongues — Spanish, Swahili, Hindi, Garifuna, Hopi, Arabic — each phrase a note in the growing chord. No translation was needed. Meaning traveled through tone.

The spirals on the ground flared white. Waves of harmonic energy rippled outward, crossing deserts, oceans, and cities. In distant laboratories, instruments erupted with unreadable data; in rural villages, radios filled with sudden, wordless music.

Across the planet, people paused mid-task — teachers, surgeons, prisoners, soldiers — and felt a stillness rise inside them, as though someone had tuned their hearts to the same frequency.

Within the field of light, Cassandra saw more than the earth. She saw patterns spiraling through galaxies, threads of consciousness stretching across dimensions. The glyph was everywhere, replicated in the movement of storms, the spin of DNA, the orbit of stars.

Nahi's voice shimmered through her.

Now you see why the song never ends.

Cassandra smiled through tears. "Then let's keep it going." She lifted her arms; the Chorus followed. Their combined tone reached a brilliance that transcended sound — pure vibration, a golden chord that folded the planet's field into alignment.

The aurora flared once more, then softened into a luminous calm.

The world exhaled.

When the light faded, they stood bathed in the quiet of completion. The sand beneath their feet glowed faintly with spiral imprints that pulsed like living veins.

Rafael looked around in awe. "It worked. The dissonance is gone."

Cassandra shook her head gently. "Not gone — balanced. Even shadow has its note in the song."

Amaru smiled. "Then we are truly the Chorus of Light."

"No," Cassandra corrected softly. "We're the Choir of Life."

That night, from the top of the Great Pyramid of Meroë, she watched the stars realign into familiar spirals. The same pattern lay within her heartbeat, and within the pulse of the earth below.

She whispered to the wind, to Nahi, to Grandma Yvette, to the countless souls who had sung before her: "The Gate remembers. The song continues."

The breeze answered in every tongue at once — the hush of waves, the murmur of trees, the laughter of children — all in perfect, living time.

Eighteen: Reflection

For three days after the Convergence, the world sang. Not metaphorically — literally. The wind carried faint harmonics where once there had been static. Trees shimmered with overtones as if chlorophyll itself were learning to hum. Seas rolled with deeper calm; even the hum of cities softened, engines syncing unconsciously to a slower rhythm.

In Neo-Meroë, thousands gathered in the streets under the golden aurora that still lingered in the sky, watching it ripple like a living breath. For the first time in generations, news networks reported *silence* as their lead story — silence that was not absence, but balance.

Across the globe, systems rebooted spontaneously. Energy grids stabilized. Patients in hospitals experienced unexplained recoveries. For seventy-two hours, every sensor that monitored the planet's electromagnetic field registered coherence — the global brain, finally in tune with itself. And at the center of it all, Cassandra felt the calm not as triumph, but as stillness before the next inhale.

She spent those days walking the dunes of Meroë barefoot, her robe gathering dust that glittered faintly with the residue of the Gate's light. The world's chatter — scientists, governments, believers, skeptics — all blurred into background. What mattered was the vibration beneath her soles: the earth's new heartbeat, steady and whole.

But on the fourth night, as she lay beneath the stars, a subtle tension returned — barely perceptible, like the faint hiss when a string goes microscopically out of tune.

She sat up, listening. At first she thought it was wind. Then she realized it was thought — billions of them. Humanity's collective mind, newly awakened, already drifting toward interpretation, ownership, categorization. The human impulse to *define* was stronger than the impulse to *listen*.

Cassandra closed her eyes, sending a single pulse of empathy outward — a gentle reminder of the spiral, of return and release. For a while, the noise subsided. But somewhere in the distance, beneath the harmony, she heard a counter tone — a low hum, deliberate, gathering mass like a storm behind the horizon.

Rafael joined her the next morning at the pyramid's edge. He carried a data pad glowing with new readings. "The resonance grids are holding," he said. "But something's... echoing back."

She glanced at the display — waveforms nearly identical to the Gate's signature, except inverted.

"A reflection?"

"Maybe. Or a resonance that doesn't want to fade," said Rafael.

Amaru arrived soon after, her shawl fluttering in the dry wind. "Balance does not erase contrast," she said softly. "It learns to dance with it."

Cassandra nodded. "Then the song isn't over."

"No," Amaru said. "It never is. But we've reached the part where memory must learn discipline."

That evening, the Chorus gathered one last time before dispersing to their homelands. They sat in a wide circle around the luminous sands, watching the aurora thin into silver twilight.

Kenji spoke quietly. "Do you think the world will stay this way?"

Cassandra looked at him, her expression both tender and resolute. "For a while. But harmony is motion. The moment we stop moving with it, dissonance will find its way back."

Rafael frowned. "You think it's already happening, don't you?"

She hesitated. The air between them quivered slightly, like a heartbeat skipping one pulse. "I believe the Gate never closes — it only reflects what we bring to it."

A soft wind circled the group, carrying a whisper of static. The aurora flickered once, faintly crimson, before settling back to gold.

No one spoke. But everyone felt it.

A reminder.
A promise.
A seed of unease wrapped in beauty.

****

Later, alone atop the pyramid, Cassandra whispered into the cooling air, "We're learning, aren't we?"

The wind responded with a sigh—neither affirmation nor denial, just continuation.

She smiled faintly. "Then we'll listen harder."

Above her, the aurora rippled once more, two spirals twisting together, one bright, one dark—ying and yang —already beginning their next dance.

And somewhere deep beneath the surface of the world, a tone rose quietly, patient as gravity.
The beginning of the next verse.

Nineteen: The Shadow Frequency

For every song that rises, an echo waits. For every light, a shadow stirs. The night after the Convergence, Cassandra dreamt not of the Temple's radiance but of distortion—its perfect geometry bending, its golden hum lowering to a growl. The once-steady pulse that had united the Chorus now trembled, as if a single discordant note had slipped into the melody.

She woke gasping. The air in her room felt *wrong*—dense, metallic, charged with static. Her lamp flickered on and off in uneven rhythm.

From the hallway, Grandma Yvette's voice called softly. "Yuh feel it too, baby?"

Cassandra nodded, whispering, "Something's... feeding."

****

Half a world away, Kenji clutched his head as hospital alarms blared. His neural monitors had spiked without cause — frequencies doubling, distorting, reversing themselves like an inverted mirror of the Gate's tone.

"Turn them off!" the nurse shouted. "They're overheating!"

But even as the machines fried, Kenji heard a whisper not from the room, but from *inside the resonance itself: The light leaves a trail. We follow the warmth.*

His breath caught. "Who are you?"

We are what the Gate forgot.

The sound fractured into laughter, low and cold.

In Peru, Amaru's fire pit, which had burned blue since the awakening, suddenly guttered out. A chill crept up her spine. She looked east and saw the stars dimming, as though a veil were being drawn across the heavens.

"They've come," she murmured.

Her apprentices found her moments later, tracing new sigils into the sand — counter-spirals meant to anchor light.

"What's happening, teacher?"

Amaru's voice was steady, though her eyes were distant. "The darkness has remembered itself."

At Meroë, the pyramids glowed faintly through the night, their energy now pulsing in irregular intervals. Dr. Dwyer watched from a distance, unease in his gut.

"These readings don't make sense," he muttered. "The resonance is collapsing in on itself, like it's being… eaten."

Merrin stared at the monitors. "Or mirrored," she said. "Every harmonic field has an anti-harmonic. Every creation has its equal opposite. Every action has its equal and opposite reaction."

Dwyer frowned. "You mean we triggered something by activating the Gate?"

Merrin did not answer. Her eyes were locked on the screens, where a new waveform had appeared, identical to Cassandra's but inverted, descending where hers ascended, a spiral of darkness against light.

"The Shadow Frequency," she whispered. "The Gate has two sides."

Cassandra saw it too, in her waking vision: a black pyramid rising beneath the golden one, its walls slick with something deeper than night. Its hum was not evil—it was *hungry*, devouring harmony and reflecting it back as dissonance.

The Guardian appeared in a shimmer of fractured light, its usual clarity dimmed.

Child of the Gate, it said, voice strained, *the shadow has answered your song. Every frequency draws its echo. This one feeds on fear, envy, and the thirst for control.*

Cassandra swallowed. "Can we stop it?"

Only by mastering the emotion it feeds upon, The Guardian assured her. *Fear unacknowledged is fuel. Fear faced is deprivation.*

She closed her eyes, feeling the tremor of panic in her chest. Around her, she could sense the Chorus—their terror flaring like sparks in a dry forest.

"We have to steady them," she said. "Before the fear spreads." She reached out across the psychic web, calling to each of them through the hum: "Kenji, breathe. Amaru, take your sandals off and ground yourself. Rafael—listen to the silence beneath the noise. We built the Gate together; we can protect it the same way." Her voice rippled across continents, a calm wave cutting through chaos.

In Japan, Kenji stilled his trembling hands.
In Peru, Amaru's fires relit, burning white this time.
In Brazil, Rafael stepped into the open air and whispered, "Reversing polarity."

Gradually, the dissonance softened. The dark pyramid faded, though not entirely. Its outline lingered beneath the earth like an afterimage.

The Guardian's voice returned, quiet but clear: *You cannot destroy it. The shadow is born with the song. But you can learn to conduct it — to turn even fear into harmony.*

Cassandra looked out over the dark desert, her reflection trembling in the window glass. "Then that's what we'll do," she said. "We'll teach the world how to sing through the dark."

And somewhere, deep beneath Meroë, the shadow pyramid pulsed once, slow, deliberate, listening.

Twenty: The Keeper's Trial

(The Descent Within)

The Shadow had grown patient. For days, it hummed beneath every conversation, a low resonance waiting at the edge of words. The world above still looked whole, still moved in rhythm, but Cassandra could feel the distortion under the surface, the tremor before the next dissonant chord. It was time to face it, not as the Keeper of the world's harmony, but as the unfinished human she still was. She told no one where she was going.

At dawn, she climbed the pyramid alone, her steps slow and deliberate, the air charged with an energy that felt like remembering. At the summit, the wind coiled around her, whispering half-phrases in the tones of the Chorus, fragments of voices and echoes of her own name, reminding her that she was the chosen helper of humankind, and it was imperative that she made the world listen.

She closed her eyes. "Show me what I've hidden."

The wind answered with silence. Then the world folded inward.

She was no longer standing on stone but in a vast chamber made of light and shadow. The walls pulsed like a living heart. In the center floated the mirror image of herself—neither fully formed nor entirely human. Its body shimmered like dark glass; within it, constellations flickered and faded.

The *other Cassandra* spoke first.

"You called me."

"I had to," Cassandra said. "The dissonance won't fade."

"Because I *am* the dissonance."

The reflection smiled faintly. "You saved the world, Keeper, but you've never forgiven yourself for surviving the accident. That guilt was the seed. You hid it beneath songs of light and called it strength."

Cassandra's hands trembled. "I was a child. In fact."

"And still are. You've built harmony by silencing the noise within you. But the noise is me—fear, pride, hunger, doubt. You tried to exile me into the field, but the field has sung me back."

Cassandra shook her head. "You feed on fear."

"No," said the shadow, stepping closer. "I *am* fear, but only because you've refused to listen."

The chamber darkened. Images burst around her — the crash, the screams, the faces of those she could not save. The guilt she thought she had healed reopened like an old wound. She fell to her knees. "I didn't mean to live when they didn't," she whispered.

The shadow knelt beside her. "Then stop meaning. Just *be*."

For a long time she wept. Not for forgiveness, but for release — the grief that had no language. Her tears hit the ground and turned into ripples of light, each one forming a spiral identical to the glyphs from Kush.

The shadow touched one of the ripples, watching it spread. "You see? We are not enemies. Only halves of a single resonance."

Cassandra lifted her gaze. The reflection looked less like darkness now and more like depth — an infinite space where light could breathe. "I built the Gate from harmony," she said slowly. "But harmony without contrast isn't music — it's monotone."

"Then play us both."

She reached out, and their hands met. Light and shadow folded together, not blending but coexisting — the two notes of a single chord.

The chamber shook. The walls dissolved into sound, a vibration that poured through her chest and into the air beyond. She felt the field — the entire global resonance — align around that tone, expanding and softening.

The Shadow did not vanish. It moved *into* her, settling like a steady pulse beneath her heartbeat. For the first time, she felt complete.

When Cassandra opened her eyes, she was back atop the pyramid. The horizon glowed faintly, neither golden nor red, but a warm bronze — the color of sunrise meeting dusk. The air was still, balanced. The world below hummed in quiet unity.

Amaru appeared beside her, though Cassandra had not heard her climb. "You found it," she said.

Cassandra nodded. "It was never lost. Just denied."

Rafael's voice crackled over the comm. "The field's stabilized. The shadow tone has merged into the base frequency. No more interference."

Cassandra smiled. "It's not interference anymore. It's the rhythm that keeps the melody alive."

Amaru studied her, eyes shining. "Then the Keeper's trial is complete."

Cassandra looked at the sky, now painted with both auroras twined together, their spirals indistinguishable. "No," she said softly. "It's begun anew. Every Keeper will face it. Every age will sing it again."

****

That evening, she wrote the last lines of her journal in the quiet of her quarters:

Harmony is not the victory of light over shadow.
It is the courage to let both exist, and still sing.

She set the stylus down and stepped outside. The desert wind was cool, carrying the faint hum of Earth—neither perfect nor broken, but breathing.

Cassandra smiled, her shadow stretching long and luminous behind her. And for the first time since the day of the crash, she felt utterly, completely human.

Twenty-One: The Chorus Reborn

D awn over Meroë was not like dawn anywhere else. It rose not only through the sky but through the *sand itself*—gold light rippling beneath the dunes as if the desert had veins of sunrise. The pyramids glowed faintly, their ancient shadows stretching toward infinity. Cassandra stood at the summit of one ruin, her arms open, eyes half-closed. She could feel them now — the Chorus — like a constellation of living stars inside her mind. Each heartbeat, each breath, pulsed in rhythm with hers. But they were flickering. The trials had begun.

The Guardian had warned her:

As you have faced your darkness, so must each who bears the song. A chorus is only harmony when every note finds its true pitch.

Kenji: The Trial of Courage

In a hospital bed in Tokyo, Kenji's monitors began to whine. His parents rushed to his side, but he was not there — not fully. His mind had descended into a corridor of mirrors where the walls replayed every moment he had been afraid to move again, every whispered pity he had overheard. In the glass before him stood the boy he used to be — strong, running, fearless.

"You can't walk," the reflection sneered. "You're broken."

Kenji clenched his fists. "No," he said softly, "I'm changing form."

He took a step forward. His reflection shattered, and when he woke, his legs tingled. Slowly, he swung them over the side of the bed and stood. The heart monitor beeped steadily, calm as music.

Thousands of miles away, Cassandra felt a pulse of triumph in her chest, and she smiled.

Amaru: The Trial of Faith

High in the Andes, Amaru knelt before a fire that refused to light. The winds howled, fierce and cold. Around her, the spirits of her ancestors gathered in the storm — faces carved of mist and thunder.

"You call yourself healer," they said, "but you doubt the medicine of your own soul."

Amaru bowed her head. "The new world no longer listens to the old ways."

"Then sing louder," the voices boomed. "Let the fire remember you."

She struck the flint again, this time humming the ancient song of balance — the same three-two rhythm of the Gate. The flame burst alive, burning pure white.

In Meroë, Cassandra inhaled sharply as Amaru's light joined hers, the link between them strengthening.

Rafael: The Trial of Logic

In São Paulo, Rafael sat surrounded by computers, data cascading across his screens in golden streams. But every equation now ended in paradox. He slammed his fists against the desk.

"This can't be real," he muttered. "It defies every law I've built my life around."

Then Cassandra's voice reached him through the hum — gentle but firm: "When numbers stop adding up, maybe it's time to listen instead of calculate."

He froze. The words were both hers and his own conscience. He looked at the chaos on his screens, took a deep breath, and stopped trying to solve the pattern. Instead, he *listened*.

The numbers began to sing. Lines of code rearranged themselves into rhythm, mathematics turning into music. He laughed out loud, tears streaming down his face. "It's not data," he whispered. "It's *harmony*."

The Global Awakening

All across the world, members of the Chorus faced their trials—each unique, yet all reflections of the same lesson. A monk in Cairo released the pride of prophecy; a scientist in Geneva surrendered the need for proof; a little girl in Kenya forgave herself for her brother's death. Their individual notes—once scattered—now resonated together, weaving a fabric of luminous sound that stretched around the planet.

Cassandra stood in the desert, eyes open to the morning light, and saw it: a shimmering aurora encircling Earth's horizon, visible even in

136

daylight. The Guardian appeared beside her, radiant and calm.

They are ready, it said. *You have tuned them, Keeper.*

"What happens now?" Cassandra asked, though she already sensed the answer.

Now the Gate no longer belongs to one. The Chorus is the Gate. Humanity itself becomes the instrument of balance.

The air thickened with resonance. Beneath their feet, the ground thrummed softly, the harmonic vibration spreading through soil and stone, through ocean currents and root systems, through the neural pathways of every living being.

In cities and villages, people paused mid-step, suddenly aware of one another—not as strangers, but as parts of a single breathing whole.

For one heartbeat, *the world aligned.*

Back at Meroë, the Chorus began to arrive in the flesh. Kenji, leaning on a cane but walking steadily. Amaru, her shawl glowing faintly with firelight. Rafael, grinning with the awe of a scientist who had met his miracle. They embraced Cassandra one by one, laughter and tears mingling in the dry desert wind.

Grandma Yvette stood a little apart, watching, pride glinting like sunlight in her eyes. "Look at yuh all," she murmured. "A song the whole world can hum."

Cassandra smiled through her tears. "We're not done yet, Grandma. The harmony's fragile. It needs an anchor."

Amaru nodded. "Then let us anchor it together."

They joined hands once more around the glowing sands of Meroë. The Guardian's voice rose like wind through strings: *The Chorus is reborn. Let the mind of Earth sing again.*

The resonance built until the air turned gold, the dunes trembling, the stars above flickering as though drawn closer by the sound.

Then came silence — profound, holy, complete. In that silence, the world breathed.

Twenty-Two: The Return Signal

Three nights later, the earth hummed like a tuning fork struck by invisible hands. Cities flickered with strange auroras, tides moved in perfect rhythm, and even the air itself seemed charged with gentle expectancy. Cassandra could feel the quiet beneath it all — an awareness, patient and vast, pressing softly against the edges of her mind. Something *was listening*.

Then, on the fourth night, the stars sang back. It began as a shimmer above Meroë, faint as breath. A single point of light blinked into being above the highest pyramid — then another, and another — until the whole sky seemed to rearrange itself into a living pattern.

Rafael was the first to notice that the constellations had changed. "They're not random," he whispered, adjusting the lenses of his field scanner. "It's the Gate's geometry — projected on a cosmic scale."

Amaru placed her palm to the sand, feeling the hum. "No, querido. It's a map. The Builders are sending us directions."

Kenji tilted his face to the sky. "They're calling us home."

Cassandra said nothing. Her pulse matched the rhythm of the light, each flash synchronizing perfectly with her heartbeat.

Then the world went silent. The wind stopped. Even the insects held their breath.

A voice, not sound but vibration, filled the air, coming from everywhere and nowhere at once.

Children of the Echo. Your song has crossed the veil.

The Chorus looked skyward as a pillar of soft white light descended, touching the ground before Cassandra. Within it shimmered symbols — spirals, waves, glyphs older than language, shifting and alive.

We are the Builders. You stand at the threshold we left behind.

The Guardian appeared beside Cassandra, kneeling slightly, its luminous wings folded. For the first time, Cassandra saw reverence in the being's movements.

They return, the Guardian whispered. *The first architects of resonance.*

The light pulsed again, the glyphs aligning into a pattern that seemed to float between thought and matter. Cassandra reached toward it instinctively.

"Can you understand them?" Rafael asked, his voice trembling.

Cassandra nodded. "Not with words. With memory." Her hand met the light, and in that instant, her consciousness stretched outward like an expanding horizon. She saw glimpses of worlds made of crystal and sound, civilizations built with harmony instead of stone, and beings who sang reality into form.

We seeded the pattern across galaxies, the Builders' voice continued. *Each world that learns balance joins the Choir of Creation. Few have reached this chord again.*

Kenji whispered, "So we're not the first?"

No. But you are the first of this age. The multiverse has waited long for Earth's return to the song.

Amaru bowed her head, tears shining in her eyes. "And what do you ask of us?"

141

To carry the resonance forward – to teach your kind that consciousness shapes the real. Fear divides. Harmony unites. The next stage is not flight through space, but awakening through self.

Cassandra's heart thrummed. "Then why do I still feel the shadow?"

The light dimmed slightly, as though sighing.

I'm surprised you have asked that, given that you've already met and merged with it. Nevertheless, you still feel it because evolution births its opposite. Every leap toward unity wakes the hunger for control. The shadow is not gone – it listens still, waiting to echo your next note. Only vigilance will keep the Gate pure.

As the Builders spoke, the Chorus's bodies began to glow with soft, living light. Not as blinding radiance, but as resonance, each frequency distinct, yet interwoven.

Rafael's instruments registered readings no machine had ever captured – energy that existed *outside measurable spectrum.*

"This is… consciousness turned tangible," he breathed. "They're showing us how thought becomes matter."

Indeed, said the Builders. *Creation is an orchestra, and every world a note. Your world has been discordant for too long. The Gate you've opened will heal more than your planet — it will tune your species to the cosmos again. We belong to a multiverse, rather than a universe.*

Suddenly, the sky flared. The light-column expanded, stretching into a shimmering corridor of starlit dust, spiraling upward into the night.

Kenji's eyes widened. "Is that — ?"

Cassandra nodded slowly. "A bridge."

The Choir awaits, said the Builders. *But the choice is yours. Cross, or remain. The Gate does not compel. It invites.*

The Chorus stood together, silent. Amaru took Cassandra's hand, her weathered fingers warm and sure.

"I will walk wherever the ancestors walk," she said.

Rafael exhaled, eyes wet. "And I'll go where the data becomes truth."

Kenji smiled shyly. "I just want to see the stars up close."

Grandma Yvette stepped forward, cane in hand. "And I'll stay. Somebody got to guard the melody down here."

Cassandra turned to her, heart swelling. "You taught me how to listen, Grandma. I'll carry that wherever I go."

Yvette nodded. "Then sing loud, baby girl. Make them remember Earth got soul."

The Guardian spread its wings, standing beside Cassandra as the starlit corridor shimmered brighter.

Go, Keeper. The Builders will show you what lies beyond the Gate. But remember — every journey outward must return within.

Cassandra turned once more to the Chorus. "Wherever we go, we go together."

And as they stepped into the light, the world around them dissolved — not into emptiness, but into harmony. The desert, the sky, the stars — all merged into a single sound so beautiful it made time stop.

The last thing Cassandra heard before crossing the threshold was her grandmother's voice carried by the wind:

144

"Keep yuh balance, Cassie. Even in Heaven."

Then the Gate folded inward, leaving only a faint echo—a hum that drifted across Earth like the softest heartbeat.

Twenty-Three: The Choir of Creation

L ight unfolded not like dawn but like thought itself — radiant, recursive, infinite. Cassandra's first breath beyond the Gate was not air but music. The sound shimmered through her being, vibrating each atom into awareness. Around her, the Chorus floated in a vast expanse that was neither space nor time, but something in between — an architecture of frequency and intention. Here, light had structure. Here, thought left footprints. Here, *existence was a song being written as it was sung.*

Kenji drifted beside her, his eyes wide with wonder. "It's... alive," he whispered.

"It's *aware*," Rafael murmured, turning in slow circles, the reflected geometry of stars dancing across his skin. "Every photon carries information; every vibration holds memory. This — this is consciousness made visible."

Amaru smiled softly. "The ancestors called this the Womb of Light. The place before beginnings."

Cassandra reached out, and light coalesced beneath her fingertips, solidifying into rippling geometry — patterns that shifted from circles to pyramids to spirals, each form humming with quiet intelligence.

Welcome, Keepers of the Gate, said the voice of the Builders. *You stand in the Choir of Creation — the living resonance that births all realities.*

The words were not sound but awareness, felt through every cell.

The Builders began to appear, their forms vast and luminous, composed of interlocking patterns of light and shadow. They moved not with steps but with changes in tone. Every gesture sent ripples through the luminous field around them.

One approached Cassandra. *Do you see now, Child of Earth, why balance is sacred? This realm is harmony itself. When imbalance arises, even thought can shatter worlds.*

Cassandra bowed her head. "And if we learn this harmony?"

147

Then you will no longer create by accident. You will create by design.

The Builders extended a hand of light toward her and said, *Touch the lattice. It will show you how consciousness weaves reality.*

Cassandra reached out again, fingers grazing the glowing web that stretched through the cosmos. Instantly, visions cascaded through her mind: galaxies spiraling into form as notes of a chord; storms born from the grief of dying stars; worlds woven by laughter, compassion, curiosity.

She saw the architecture of thought—how emotion and imagination, when aligned, became the raw fabric of existence.

Each mind, the Builders said, *is a filament in this vast harmony. Most species live unaware that their dreams sculpt the world. But your kind... your kind has begun to remember.*

Kenji laughed in delight. "Then Earth was never separate—it was just one verse in the song."

Yes, the Builders replied. *But a verse that almost forgot its rhythm.*

Amaru's shawl shimmered into new colors as she floated nearer the lattice. "How do we keep the balance now that we know?"

By teaching others to listen. By showing that fear distorts, but love refines.

Rafael frowned thoughtfully. "Love as a measurable frequency?"

The Builders' voices resonated together, harmonious and precise, *Love is not sentiment — it is coherence. The unbroken alignment between thought, emotion, and being. Every act of creation born from coherence sustains life. Every act born from division unravels it.*

Cassandra absorbed every vibration, every image. The knowledge was not learned; it *unfolded* inside her. "So creation is continuous," she said quietly. "Every breath, every word, every idea builds or breaks the harmony."

Exactly, Keeper. That is the power — and the peril — of consciousness.

Then the light dimmed slightly, revealing a horizon of cascading golden waves. The Builders gestured toward it. *This is the Choir itself — the heart of all harmonies. It sings the memory of what was, and the promise of what may yet be.*

From within the waves rose voices — millions, billions — singing in chords too vast for comprehension. The sound was at once joyful and mournful, creation and loss intertwined.

Cassandra's chest tightened with awe. "It's beautiful."

It is everything, said the Builders. *But the Choir changes when new voices join. Will you add yours?*

The Chorus looked to Cassandra. She nodded once. "We're ready."

Together, they closed their eyes and began to sing — not with words, but with will. Their tones rose like dawn through the field of light, merging with the ancient song of the Builders. Their voices carried memories of Earth — the laughter of children, the rhythm of rain, the heartbeat of the ocean, the quiet resilience of humanity. The Choir absorbed it all, expanding, brightening, shimmering with new color.

Earth has rejoined the harmony, the Builders said, their tones now glowing with warmth. *Your song will echo across galaxies. You have remembered what many forgot — that consciousness is not bound by flesh or planet. It is the light that sings itself into form.*

Cassandra felt herself dissolve — not dying, but *becoming.* The boundaries of her body faded as her awareness merged with the music. She felt every star as a pulse, every atom as a chord, every soul as a lyric.

And through it all, one thread remained — Grandma Yvette's voice, carried across dimensions, whispering in rhythm with the cosmic song: "Sing true, Cassie. Sing home."

The Builders' final message resonated through the Choir: *Go now, Keepers. You have learned the architecture of creation. Use it wisely. Teach it humbly. Remember — light is eternal, but harmony must be renewed with every breath.*

The light around them shimmered once more, the Choir fading into the horizon of sound.

When Cassandra opened her eyes again, she stood once more in the golden sands of Meroë. The pyramids glowed faintly. The Chorus stood beside her, silent, radiant, forever changed.

No one spoke. They did not need to. The song lived within them now.

Above them, the stars pulsed softly—each one a note in the endless music of becoming.

Twenty-Four: The Return to Earth

For a long moment—or perhaps a thousand years—Cassandra floated in silence. No light, no sound, only the steady hum of existence itself. Then, like breath filling new lungs, reality unfolded around her. The golden tones of the Choir faded, replaced by a different sound—*wind*. Hot, dry, real. She opened her eyes. Meroë.

The dunes looked the same at first glance, but the air was... heavier. The pyramids, once half-buried in sand, now gleamed with strange metal reinforcements, their geometry humming faintly with modern machinery. Cassandra blinked, steadying herself. "How long...?"

Rafael was beside her, his face older somehow, streaked with silver though only minutes had seemed to pass. Kenji and Amaru stirred nearby, each of them carrying the same faint aura of ageless light.

From the horizon came a distant roar—a craft, sleek and silver, descending on pillars of blue flame.

"It's Earth," Rafael said softly, scanning the skyline where towers pierced the haze. "But not the one we left."

They stood together as the craft touched down. A hatch hissed open, releasing a rush of sterile, cool air. Figures emerged—humanoid, draped in robes interwoven with circuitry, eyes glowing faintly gold. One of them stepped forward, studying Cassandra with awe.

"Welcome back," the figure said in a soft, modulated voice. "You're standing in the Central Sahara Sovereign Zone—formerly Sudan. The pyramids of Meroë are now sacred monuments of the Resonance Age."

"The what?" Kenji asked, eyes wide.

The figure smiled gently. "It has been one hundred and seventy-three years since the Gate first sang. Humanity calls it *The Awakening*."

Cassandra's heart stopped. "A century and a half?"

"Time," Rafael murmured, "moves differently in the Choir's field. We've crossed a harmonic interval."

Amaru touched the sand reverently. "The world grew while we were gone."

The guide—if that's what they were—gestured toward the horizon. "Much of the planet now lives by the Law of Coherence. Cities are built upon resonance grids. Energy flows without fuel. Illnesses respond to harmonic recalibration. But…"

The pause lingered.

"But?" Cassandra prompted.

"Not all remembered balance," the guide said quietly. "A faction calling itself the *Sons of Dissonance* rejects the harmony. They weaponize the frequencies—turn them into tools of dominance."

Kenji swallowed. "The Shadow Frequency."

Rafael's brow furrowed. "It survived."

Amaru looked toward Cassandra. "So, our work is not done."

Cassandra nodded slowly. "The Gate gave humanity the song—but it can't make them sing in tune."

They followed the guide into the city that rose beyond the dunes. The architecture was breathtaking—organic shapes fused with light, structures that pulsed like living instruments. People moved gracefully, their voices calm, their gestures synchronized with invisible rhythm.

But beneath the serenity, Cassandra felt an undertone—a dissonant hum, faint yet persistent, like a crack in crystal. Children laughed nearby, playing with spheres of glowing sound that floated at their command. One looked up at Cassandra, eyes wide with recognition. "You're from the First Chorus," he whispered. "The Keeper."

Cassandra knelt, smiling gently. "You remember the old songs?"

The boy nodded. "In our dreams. But some people say they're just myths."

Cassandra's heart ached. "Then it's time to remind them."

As dusk fell, the Chorus stood atop a terrace overlooking the reimagined Meroë. The city's lights pulsed in slow, coordinated rhythm, like a sleeping organism breathing through circuits and stars.

Rafael spoke first. "They've built paradise — and yet, I can still hear the tension. It's mathematical. Two frequencies, close but never converging."

Amaru nodded. "Harmony without humility breeds its own imbalance."

Cassandra closed her eyes. Through the hum of civilization, she could feel it — the same old tremor that once lurked beneath her heartbeat: fear disguised as control.

"The Sons of Dissonance," she whispered. "They're amplifying the Shadow Frequency again."

Kenji turned to her, his expression both fearful and resolute. "Then we need to retune the world."

That night, the stars shimmered differently — brighter, closer. The Gate still pulsed faintly above the Earth's magnetic field, visible now as an aurora that never set.

157

Cassandra stood at the edge of the terrace, her hair stirred by the warm wind. She placed her hand over her heart and felt the vibration still within her, stronger than ever.

"They learned to sing," she said softly. "Now they must learn to *listen*."

Amaru approached, resting a hand on her shoulder. "Then we teach them, Keeper. Not as gods, but as reminders."

Cassandra smiled. "The Builders gave us the architecture. Now we build the harmony."

And as she spoke, the sky above the new Earth flickered—a faint pulse of shadow twisting through the aurora like a warning tremor.

The Guardian's voice, distant but clear, whispered across the wind: *The melody continues, but so does the echo. Be ready, Cassandra. Every harmony calls forth its next dissonance.*

Cassandra gazed toward the horizon, where old dunes met new towers, ancient Earth met living light.

"Then let the next song begin," she whispered.

Twenty-Five: The Sons of Dissonance

The hum of the new world had a fracture. To most, it sounded like background noise — barely audible beneath the steady pulse of the planetary resonance grids. But to Cassandra, it was unmistakable: the rhythm was off by one infinitesimal beat. The harmony humanity had inherited was drifting. That was how she found them — the *Sons of Dissonance.* They lived beneath the music, hidden in the sublevels of cities built on sound. Their frequencies cloaked them from detection; their language was static, their creed — *"Control the chord, control creation."*

Cassandra and Rafael entered the undercity of Neo-Meroë disguised as engineers, their bodies cloaked in dampeners to mute their auras. Rows of machines thrummed softly, filtering the world's resonance into dense, black conduits. The air smelled of copper and ozone. The further they descended, the colder it became.

Kenji's voice crackled through their mind link. *"They're tracing you. Three signals closing in."*

"Let them," Cassandra replied silently. "I need to see their core."

They stepped into an immense hall—a cathedral of inverted light. Massive harmonic stabilizers pulsed along the walls, feeding into a central spire that glowed with dark crimson. The resonance was not golden here—it was angular, jagged, angry. And standing at the center, directing the frequencies with elegant precision, was a man Cassandra recognized instantly.

"*Rafael?*" she whispered.

Rafael froze beside her, eyes wide.

"No," he breathed. "It can't be."

The figure turned. His face was older, harder— but familiar in every line. It was *Rafael*, or rather, another version of him.

"Welcome, Cassandra Clairborne," the other Rafael said, his voice both human and mechanical, reverberating in two tones. "We've been expecting you."

160

Her companion stepped forward. "Who are you?"

"I am what you would have become had you chosen control over compassion," said the echo of Rafael. "When we crossed the Choir, not all of us returned clean. Some fragments of consciousness lingered in the shadow field. I... evolved there."

Amaru's voice whispered through the link. *"The Shadow made a twin of him — a reflection sustained by imbalance."*

"Why?" Cassandra asked. "Why twist the harmony?"

The doppelgänger smiled faintly. "Because balance without authority is chaos. Humanity sings in tune, yes — but who decides the melody? Someone must conduct the orchestra."

At a signal from his hand, the hall vibrated violently. Images flared along the walls: cities governed by resonance algorithms, people moving like synchronized drones.

"This," the false Rafael said, "is coherence perfected. No conflict. No deviation. Harmony achieved through control."

"That's not harmony," Cassandra said sharply. "That's silence."

He tilted his head. "Silence is the purest sound."

Her anger rose, but beneath it pulsed something deeper — sorrow. The man before her was still part of the same melody; a verse that had gone flat.

"You're feeding on the Shadow Frequency," she said quietly. "It's using you."

He smiled. "Or *I* am using it. Doesn't matter. Either way, the world listens when I speak."

Cassandra reached inward, calling to the Chorus. Instantly, she felt them — Amaru grounding from afar, Kenji lending courage, Grandma Yvette's distant voice humming like prayer. Her eyes glowed softly. "You've mistaken unity for obedience. Harmony isn't sameness; it's relationship."

"Spoken like a dreamer," the doppelgänger replied. "Let me show you reality."

The spire blazed, and a shockwave of inverted resonance burst outward. Cassandra screamed as frequencies tore through her mind, showing visions of cities collapsing under sound, oceans resonating into chaos.

The shadow Rafael approached her through the storm. "You can't stop me. You built this world's song—I merely changed the key."

Cassandra steadied herself, pushing through the distortion. "Then I'll remind it what key it's meant to be in."

She slammed her palms together, releasing a golden tone that split the darkness like lightning. The resonance walls cracked, the spire flickered, and for one blinding instant, light and shadow harmonized.

Then—silence.

When the echoes cleared, the dark Rafael was gone, the spire dormant. Only his voice lingered, ghostly and soft: *"You can delay dissonance, Cassandra. You can't erase it. Every melody needs contrast—or it fades into noise."*

Cassandra fell to her knees, trembling. Rafael—the real one—caught her, his eyes full of sorrow.

"He's right about one thing," she said through gritted teeth. "We can't erase dissonance."

"But?" he asked.

She looked up, her gaze fierce. "We can teach the world to *compose with it.*"

As they emerged from the undercity, dawn broke across the new earth. The hum of the resonance grids was steady again—but Cassandra knew it was fragile.

Amaru met them at the gate, her shawl rippling in the wind. "Have you seen what lies below?"

"Yes," Cassandra said. "And it's only the beginning."

She looked toward the rising sun, feeling both the ache and the hope of what was to come.

"The next song," she whispered, "will have to include the shadow."

And the world, listening, seemed to tremble in agreement.

Twenty-Six: The Second Gate

It began as a whisper on the edge of the resonance grid, a low, warping vibration too deep for machines to measure but powerful enough to make the ground tremble. Within weeks, the hum spread. Entire cities along the equatorial line flickered with static in the resonance streams. The aurora that had once been soft and golden now bled into deep crimson bands twisting through the upper atmosphere.

Rafael called it *feedback.*
Amaru called it *a wound.*
Cassandra knew it for what it was—*a mirror.*

The failed spire of the Sons of Dissonance had become the seed of a new threshold. A *Second Gate.*

Satellite telemetry showed the rift blooming over the Indian Ocean like a dark halo—an inversion of the original Gate's radiant geometry. Where the first had sung, this one *screamed.*

The frequencies of fear, greed, and obsession gathered there, bending energy inward until even light seemed to hesitate near it.

At the Council of Resonance in Neo-Meroë, Cassandra stood before the world's delegates. "This is no natural phenomenon," she said, her voice steady. "It's an echo created by imbalance. The first Gate opened through harmony. This one feeds on distortion."

The hall fell silent except for the pulsing hum in the distance — the planet itself vibrating out of tune. A diplomat rose. "Then close it, Keeper. Isn't that your power?"

Cassandra shook her head. "The Gate doesn't obey power. It responds to consciousness. We can't destroy it from without. We have to *enter it.*"

****

THAT NIGHT, THE CHORUS GATHERED for the first time in decades. Those who had once sung the first Gate into being, were now older, wiser, and wary.

Kenji stood beside a transport drone, his once-youthful face marked with lines of quiet purpose. "So we're diving into a black hole made of thought?" he asked wryly.

Rafael adjusted his gauntlet of harmonic sensors. "Not a black hole—a mirror frequency. If we can map its pattern, we can counter-tune it."

Amaru spread her shawl, revealing sigils of gold and obsidian woven into the fabric. "Balance must be restored at the root, not the reflection."

Cassandra placed a hand over her heart. "The Second Gate was born from humanity's shadow. If we don't meet it there, it will consume everything we've built."

They formed a circle once more, hands clasped as the sky roared above them. The aurora had split now—half light, half shadow—two songs competing for dominion.

The Gate awaits, whispered the Guardian from somewhere between worlds. *But remember, Keeper, the dark does not deceive. It reflects.*

Their vessel—an inter-resonant craft woven from living light—rose into the storm. At the edge of the rift, the air thickened, color bending inward until reality itself seemed to fold.

Cassandra felt her heart synchronize with the rhythm of the distortion. "It's... calling us," she murmured.

Kenji gripped the controls. "Then let's answer before it decides to call something else."

The ship entered the vortex.

Instantly, the world inverted. Sound became shape. Light became pressure. Time unraveled like silk.

They were not traveling through space; they were moving through *emotion*. Every fear humanity had ever felt, every selfish act, every unhealed wound manifested as waves of chaotic resonance pressing against them.

Rafael's instruments overloaded. "The frequency density is off the charts. If we don't stabilize soon—"

Cassandra raised her hand. "Stop fighting it."

"What?"

"Let it show us what we're resisting."

The ship shuddered. Darkness peeled back to reveal scenes—cities burning from ambition, oceans rising with neglect, children crying beneath the static of false perfection. Humanity's shadow played out in raw, unfiltered sound and color.

Cassandra closed her eyes. "This is our collective noise."

Amaru's voice broke through the roar. "Then quiet it, child. Not with silence — *with truth.*"

Cassandra began to hum — the tone of the original Gate. One by one, the others joined her, their frequencies blending into counterpoint. The chaos around them slowed, its jagged edges smoothing into rhythm.

Then, from the heart of the darkness, a figure emerged — glowing faintly red, eyes bright as coals. It was *him* — the dark Rafael, the echo she had thought dispersed. "You can't erase what you denied," he said. "The Gate isn't your enemy. It's your teacher."

Cassandra met his gaze. "Then teach me."

He reached out his hand, and for a heartbeat, the two harmonics collided — light and dark spiraling together until they became indistinguishable.

Cassandra saw everything: the first resonance, the fall, the rebuilding, and the endless cycle between harmony and dissonance.

Balance was not stasis; it was motion. The Gate was not evil; it was the necessary echo that made the song complete.

She extended both hands, merging her tone with his.

The Second Gate flared.

Across the planet, resonance grids trembled, then realigned. The crimson aurora softened into silver-gold. The frequencies that had split now overlapped, forming a single pulse that carried through air, ocean, and soul.

Cassandra opened her eyes inside the vortex, light streaming from every pore. "Not two gates," she whispered. "One song."

The dark Rafael smiled faintly as his form began to fade. "Then you've learned the final verse."

When the Chorus emerged, the storm was gone. The world was quiet—still humming, but softer, balanced.

Rafael looked at Cassandra, awe in his eyes. "You merged them."

"No," she said gently. "They merged themselves. We just listened."

Amaru bowed her head. "And so ends the discord."

Cassandra turned toward the horizon where dawn shimmered across the ocean. "No," she said softly. "It's not an ending. It's the tuning before the next song."

The Guardian's voice echoed like wind through glass: *Harmony restored. The Gate whole. The Keeper's duty fulfilled.*

But Cassandra knew better. Balance, once found, must always be kept.

Twenty-Seven: The Reclamation

The hum of the world was gentle again. No longer a roar, no longer silence, just the steady rhythm of balance breathing through everything that lived.

In the years after the Second Gate, the planet learned to sing in a new way. Cities that once glowed with rigid precision now pulsed with organic rhythm; music was not only art but architecture. Farmers tuned their crops to harmonic resonance, oceans responded to collective meditation, and children were taught early that thought was a tool to heal, not to conquer. At the center of this quiet renaissance stood Cassandra Clairborne—the Keeper of Balance.

The Academy of Resonance sat on the same desert plateau where the pyramids of Meroë had first awakened the Gate. Its courtyards were paved with crystal sand that shimmered like frozen sunlight, and its halls hummed softly, alive with the voices of students learning to weave intention into vibration.

Cassandra moved among them not as a goddess, but as a teacher, barefoot, simple, smiling. Her presence was calm but vast, like standing beside the ocean at dusk. She paused by a group of children gathered around a harmonic sphere. The orb shifted colors as they laughed and argued over the right tone to stabilize it.

One boy frowned. "I can't keep it still, Miss Cassie! It keeps changing."

Cassandra knelt beside him, placing her hand on the sphere. The colors steadied instantly, glowing gold. "That's because you're trying to make it obey you," she said gently. "You can't force harmony. You invite it."

The boy's eyes widened. "Like… asking it to play with me?"

She smiled. "Exactly. Harmony doesn't follow — it dances."

Later, as twilight spread across the dunes, Cassandra climbed to the terrace overlooking the desert. The horizon shimmered with light from thousands of resonance beacons, each one a song point connecting the planet's frequencies.

Amaru joined her, her shawl now embroidered with symbols from every culture of the new age. Her eyes were bright with both pride and age.

"You've done it, niña," she said softly. "You turned the song of one soul into the music of all humanity."

Cassandra's gaze remained on the horizon. "Not only *me*, *we* did. The world just needed to remember what it already knew."

Amaru chuckled. "And what will you do when the next discord arises?"

Cassandra smiled faintly. "Listen first. Then sing louder, harmonizing each note to merge with the melody."

At night, she often sat beneath the stars, her thoughts wandering to those who had shaped her path: Grandma Yvette, whose laughter had once steadied her; Kenji, now an ambassador teaching resonance medicine in Japan; Rafael, whose redeemed brilliance had become the foundation of planetary science; and Amaru, who guided the cultural harmonics of entire nations.

But sometimes, when the desert was quiet enough, she could still hear the Guardian's voice carried on the wind:

The melody endures, Keeper. Remember — every child born hears the first note of creation. Teach them to keep it pure.

She would close her eyes and whisper, "Always."

Decades passed. Cassandra grew older, though the light within her never dimmed. When she walked, the sands beneath her feet vibrated softly, echoing her heartbeat. People came from every continent to hear her speak, but her lessons were always the same — simple, human, and eternal:

"Balance is not perfection. It's participation."
"Harmony is not the absence of conflict; it's the courage to listen through it."
"And power without wisdom is noise."

One dawn, she returned to the pyramids of Meroë alone. The first sun of the new century burned gold against the horizon. She placed her hand on the cool stone and felt the hum of the original Gate beneath it—steady, alive.

"The song continues," she whispered.

Behind her, a group of young students approached, their laughter light in the morning air. One girl carried a crystal sphere glowing faintly pink. "Teacher," she called, "will you show us how to make the colors sing together?"

Cassandra turned, her smile soft as the wind. "No," she said. "*You'll* show me."

The children laughed, circling her as they began to hum. Their voices rose in unison, imperfect but joyous, each one distinct yet part of the same living chord.

As their music filled the desert, Cassandra lifted her gaze to the sky, where the faint shimmer of the Gate still hung like a memory of light. She no longer needed to reach for it. It was already within her—and within them. When she finally closed her eyes, the Guardian's voice came one last time, warm as sunrise:

You began as a child who survived. You became the Keeper who remembered. And now you are the note that never fades.

Cassandra smiled, whispering into the quiet,
"The mind is the temple. The light is the door.
But love—love is the song."

And the world sang with her.

Epilogue: The Legacy of the Keeper

Centuries passed like gentle breaths through a well-tuned instrument. The Academy of Resonance had grown into a living organism—its crystalline walls vibrating softly with the low hum of the planet's pulse. Where once scholars came to measure sound, they now came to understand silence. Cassandra taught from no podium; she sat among her students beneath the open sky, letting the wind be the first voice in every lesson.

On this morning, she traced two spirals in the sand—one bright, one dark—letting them touch at the center. "This," she said, her voice calm and resonant, "is the heart of the Gate. Two notes, not in competition but in conversation. The world breathes between them."

A young Keeper-in-training, a girl about the age Cassandra had been when the accident changed everything, asked quietly, "Which one

178

are we meant to follow—the light or the shadow?"

Cassandra smiled. "Neither. You follow the space between. The song lives there."

The girl nodded slowly, understanding without words, and began to hum a low tone. Others joined—different pitches, imperfect, human. The combined sound lifted into the air, carried by warmth, rising like prayer and laughter intertwined.

Cassandra closed her eyes and listened. The melody wove through her like memory: the crash, the pyramid, Nahi's touch, the Gate's awakening, the Shadow's return—all part of the same unending chord. She whispered, barely audible, "Every Keeper must learn to play both."

Above them, the aurora shimmered in gold and crimson, no longer divided but braided together like threads of one eternal tapestry.

Cassandra breathed deeply, her heart aligned with the rhythm of Earth. The wind answered in a soft counter-melody, and for a moment, she felt the multiverse smile.

Then she joined her students' song, her voice neither leader nor echo, but harmony itself, the

space between the ying and the yang — the
Keeper of Two Chords, teaching the world to
balance its own beautiful noise.

About the Author

George P A Dover is an author, publisher, language arts professor, spoken-word artist, and the CEO of Olai Multiversal Enterprises LLC and Global Elite Force Security, Inc. Over the years, he has earned many awards, including a Government of Guyana academic scholarship to Cuba, a CMP Media Journalism Award, a Stony Brook Southampton College scholarship for a master of arts in creative writing, and a joint scholastic editor award as Features Editor of Pandora's Box, the official student newspaper of York College of CUNY. His work spans newspapers, magazines, television, radio, and many internet platforms. He currently lives in Southern California with his lovely family.